WIDE EYED

STORIES BY
TRINIE DALTON

AKASHIC BOOKS
NEW YORK

Published by Akashic Books
©2005 Trinie Dalton

ISBN-13: 978-1-888451-86-5
ISBN-10: 1-888451-86-6
Library of Congress Control Number: 2005925470
First printing
Printed in Canada

Some of these stories were also published in the following places: *Santa Monica Review*, *Purple*, *Textfield*, *Frozen Tears* (anthology), *Fishwrap*, *K48*, *Ab/Ovo* (exhibition catalogue), *Swivel*, *Suspect Thoughts Magazine*, *Bennington Review*, *Court Green*, *The Dogs* (exhibition catalogue), *Bomb*, *Punk Planet*, and *Lost on Purpose* (anthology).

The title "The Tide of My Mounting Sympathy" was borrowed from Wayne C. Booth's phrase "the tide of our mounting sympathy" from his critical essay "Macbeth as Tragic Hero."

"Extreme Sweets" borrows Laura from *The Glass Menagerie* by Tennessee Williams.

Little House on the Bowery
c/o Akashic Books
PO Box 1456
New York, NY 10009
Akashic7@aol.com
www.akashicbooks.com

For Matt Greene
and the Daltons

ACKNOWLEDGMENTS

Sincerest thanks to: Mike Bauer, Molly Bendall, Jesse Bransford, Sue de Beer, Martha Cooley, Roman Coppola, Sean Dungan, David Gates, Amanda Greene, David Hamma, Amy Hempel, Annie Heringer, Lisa Wagner Holley, Peter Kim, Rachel Kushner, Jill McCorkle, Casey McKinney, KC Mosso, Heidi Nelms, Shuggie, David St. John, Gail Swanlund, Johnny Temple, Andrew Tonkovich, Joel Westendorf, and Yucca.

Thanks to Benjamin Weissman and Amy Gerstler for being the ultimate teachers and friends.

Thanks to Dennis Cooper for this book.

TABLE OF CONTENTS

DECREPIT

I'd want a range life
If I could settle down.
If I could settle down,
Then I would settle down.
—Pavement

We were performing a play about this maggot on our kitchen floor who grew until he was squishing out the windows, suffocating us and all those who came into the Ranch House.

The maggot play was meant to be retro, like *Godzilla* or *King Kong*—one of those huge-creatures-dominating-humanity stories. But we were wasted on Xanax, dressed in red dresses and red feather boas, so it had a New Wave feel.

"Don't eat me, you maggot," I said to the two-foot-long papier-mâché maggot lying on the floor.

"I vill crush you," said Heidi, in a low, Kruschevian

maggot/dictator voice from behind the door. "I am zee maggot."

That's the only part I remember. The script was pathetic.

Heidi, Annie, and I—roommates—renamed the *Blue* House the *Ranch* House. It was a one-story, spread out, casual Craftsman-style place.

Everything was decrepit: termites ruined the walls and vines grew in the windows. We spent our time learning Carter Family songs. Sara and Maybelle are easier to imitate than A.P.'s baritone parts. I can still play "Single Girl," "Wandering Boy," and "Wildwood Flower" on guitar. We had pie parties and sang to guys we invited over to eat elderberry pie hot out of the oven. The elderberries came from trees in the park because we had no money to buy grocery store ones. Countryfolk wannabes for sure.

My first night in that house I raided the basement and found a shawl, rusty tools, and knitting equipment. I had a spooky meeting with the ghost of the old lady who died there. She was making the rooms cold. Drafts of winter air were leaking through sealed windowsills even though it was summer. I told her to leave because three girls were moving in. I was alone and sensed her in the corner of the den, rocking in her invisible rocking chair. I heard the chair creaking and could smell the stale scent of the elderly. She'd died in the 1970s and no one had lived there since, the realtor told me. It made sense, then, that someone should tell her to beat it.

Back when I was nine my aunt told me that to get rid of a poltergeist, I should be firm. It really works. The Ranch House Ghost departed that night. Our theory was that she'd been buried under the avocado tree in the backyard. It had years of leaf debris piled beneath it, and grew avocados the size of cantaloupes. We figured the human compost had beefed them up. Also, next to the tree was a defunct incinerator— convenient. Her son must have folded her up, shoved her in, fired up the stove, and burned her into an ashen pile, ideal for fertilizer. That's why our tree kicked ass.

There are a lot of ghosts and good avocado trees in The Echo Park. I didn't know there was a "the" before Echo Park until I went to the local liquor store, House of Spirits, to get tequila for our "ranchwarming" party. I was talking to the lady behind the counter, telling her I'd just moved back into the neighborhood.

"It's the only place I feel at home," I said.

"So many kinds of people. Less old people now. They're all dying," she said.

I knew she meant the Echo Park Convalescent Home down the street, where heaps of old people roll around in wheelchairs and smell everything up. No one likes that haunted house.

The guys behind me in line started in.

"You used to live somewhere else?" one asked. He looked tight in his L.A. Dodgers cap, oversized white T-shirt, Dickies shorts, and Nike Cortez sneakers, with white tube socks pulled up over his calves. All his friends looked the same and had shaved heads.

"Yeah. But I missed stuff, like kids setting off fireworks. Or wild dogs," I said.

"You always come back to The Echo Park," he said. "You can't ever leave The Echo Park." He nodded his head at my tequila bottle.

I saw a dead body while I was living in the Ranch House. Not in the house, down a couple miles in the donut store parking lot. I was walking by, and there was yellow tape all around as if the cops thought people were going to poke the body or something. It was lying in a conspicuously contorted position, legs bent in wrong directions, neck turned too far over. Man, middle-aged. No blood. Almost like he'd been pushed out of the passenger seat by someone driving at high speed and rolled all the way into the parking lot. I associated the body with the donuts and haven't eaten there since. After all, Ms. Donut is right around the corner. It's the feminist donut shop.

"What kind of life would you have if you could change yours?" Heidi asked me one afternoon while she washed potatoes in the sink.

I stood leaning on the doorjamb. "A range life," I said. That was my favorite song. I'd drink gin on the porch and listen to it. I'd gaze at the corn we planted where the lawn used to be and think about settling down. "Why?" I continued. "You sick of me? Just because I refrigerate butter?" Heidi left it out on the counter in a country-style butter dish. I hate soft, hot butter.

"Remember when the cats attacked it?" she asked. Her green gingham apron was spotted with potato bits.

It was Easter morning. We were out hunting colored eggs under the avocado tree. When we shooed the cats away, there was this little pile of butter scalloped into a pyramid shape by lick marks from their sandpapery tongues. Land O' Lakes, unsalted—with the box where you can tear off the Indian princess and fold her knees into her chest area so she has major hooters.

There were two rules of the house: wear clothes only when necessary, and always burn candles and incense to appease spirits. Nudity made us feel closer to those in nether-regions. Bare skin seemed more ghosty. We weren't trying to attract ghosts, but we respected them. The Old Lady Ghost was gone, but we still smelled her occasionally. I'd catch a whiff when I opened the medicine cabinet or stepped into the laundry room. She smelled like the nursing home, like musty sweaters and dirty flannel sheets. Ghosts smell pretty much the same as those about to die—which is totally separate from the way dead bodies smell. Ghosts aren't rotten, but there is a hint of putrefaction that makes me aware of their status: not dead yet, or already dead and separated from the physical body. Why don't ghosts smell fresh and young? Maybe old people don't remember how they smelled as kids so neither can ghosts.

* * *

There was another old lady next door, alive but barely. She grew candy-striped beets and okra in her front yard. Yet she didn't smell like she was dying. She prided herself on her odorless house.

"I hate bad smells," she said as she gave the three of us a tour of her house one day. It was a Craftsman-style too, stained dark wood inside, black velvet curtains over the windows. The bank was threatening to take it from her. "Your house smells," she added.

"Just that one time," I said. Some zucchinis in the crisper had gone bad. "Myrna, what can get candle wax out of carpet?" A votive candle had burned all night, tipped over, and run between the carpet hairs in our living room.

"An iron and a dish towel," she said. She showed us the method, making ironing movements in midair.

We fell asleep huddled on the floor around a candle because my mom called and was having visions of a murderer living next door to us, waiting to strike. My mom had psychic powers that we took pretty seriously, not seriously enough to move out that night as she had requested, but seriously enough to burn extra candles and incense, and to keep all the doors locked with the cats inside.

"Why is there so much spiritual drama here?" Annie asked that night. We listened to *Let It Bleed* by the Rolling Stones while locked in.

"Welcome to Echo Park," Heidi said. I thought again of that old folks' home down the block, and pictured their garden filled with car exhaust–coated agapanthus and weedy impatiens, barely tended to. The institutional garden, devoid of love.

"Do you two ever get a bad feeling when you walk past that convalescent hospital?" I asked. I kept thinking of that awful place. I took it as a sign, but I didn't know of what.

"No, except that everyone there's going to die," said Heidi.

"Maybe all their fears combine and rub off on you," Annie said.

That night I dreamt I was Sara Carter. I was dressed in raggedy clothes and holey leather shoes. The next day I tried to write a song about Echo Park, about how when I'm about to die I hope people will bring me back and bury me . . . but not under an old willow tree. Where then? In Echo Park Lake, under the lotus flowers littered with McDonald's wrappers and devoured cobs of corn? Further down Alvarado Street in MacArthur Park, where so many dead bodies are dredged out of the lake? Would I be buried under the aptly named House of Spirits? *None of these places are worthy of my corpse*, I thought. Just as in the old ballads, I want to be buried by the seashore or under some significant tree.

We got evicted from the Ranch House when the bank bought it. Shortly before we got kicked out, our dog died, which was the first sign of things winding down. Then Myrna, our neighbor, declared bankruptcy and lost her house. The third sign was when our friend Melissa moved out of her house up the street because she kept hearing machine gun noises on the ground floor. She found out that her house had been a gangster hideout during the bootlegging era—lots of people died in it. My mom was hospitalized for hearing voices. A gardener chopped down our avocado tree.

I wanted to be buried under that tree, with the cremated Old Lady. It's the only place that comes to mind when I think of drafting a will. I'd like to be charred in that very incinerator, but I don't think the guy who lives there now would allow it. I've driven by and seen him on several occasions watering his lawn where our corn used to be.

The Carter Sisters are like ghosts, singing about the space between heaven and hell. *Do not disturb / My waking dream / The splendor of / That winding stream.* That land doesn't seem to include Los Angeles, or anywhere west of the Mississippi. I worry that I come from a place with so few legends, or, to be more accurate, legends that are speculative. Big deal—old ladies, gangsters, tequila, banks taking houses away from people, people getting killed in front of donut shops. There's no real way to know the other people who lived in these rented houses, apart from rummaging through what they left in basements then concocting harebrained ghost stories about them.

On the nights I lie awake wondering where to be buried, I sometimes recall staring up at the Ranch House's stuccoed ceiling—the plaster sparkled with glitter. I'd wake up in the middle of the night imagining it to be the night sky. A burning candle made it twinkle even more. It was disco and country at the same time—glam-rural—a combo that makes me realize the irony of a band called Pavement singing about Range Life. I know I'll be an old lady ghost because I lie in bed feeling young and old at the same time. Young in experience, but old because I wish to be part of some tradition. I crave a past but don't want to live in it. Eras run into one ageless mess. Ghosts live in different times simultaneously. They yearn for what's lost. I haven't even lost anything but I still find myself yearning for it. Not knowing where you come from is dumber than never wanting to leave.

HUMMINGBIRD MOONSHINE

The Summer of Ailments sucked. Nerve pain extended from my ass down the length of my left leg. I walked heavily on my right leg, so that my right foot developed calluses. I bought a specially padded pair of sneakers but my feet got hot and unbearably smelly, and I had to throw them out. Hangnails plagued me. A sunburn turned into a skin cancer, and the doctor left laser scars on my chest when he removed it. My eyes were tired from reading too much. I had a broken rib from slipping on the edge of a pool at a barbecue. At the dog park, an Akita bit me—I got stitches that ran from the tip of my forefinger to the base of my thumb. The stitch-line got sunburned, which made it puffy with infection.

Friends told me that simultaneous injuries meant good luck because I'd used up all my bad luck at once. *How much worse can it get?* I wondered. *Am I cursed? Who would have cursed me?*

I made a trip downtown to the Million Dollar Pharmacia, a botanica full of folk curatives, para-phernalia for casting spells, incense, candles, charms, and portraits of the saints. I'd been there many times before to buy votive candles with Buena Suerte prayers printed on them. *Fast Money Blessing, Law—Stay Away!*, and *The Omnipresence of God* were the most recent candles I'd burned. I also stocked up on La Chuparrosa stuff, anything with a hummingbird on it. "Song of the Chuparrosa" came printed on a box of hummingbird soap, here translated from Spanish:

Oh divine hummingbird!
You who sucks the nectar of the flowers!
You who gives life to women in love!
I rely on you—I am a sinner.
Your powerful fluids protect me and provide me
With the faculties to control myself as well as to experi-
ence enjoyment.
I keep you in my saint's locket so I may walk with you,
My beautiful hummingbird.

Recite this prayer on Thursdays and Sundays,
with a lit candle, while imagining her.

After my boyfriend Matt saved a hummingbird's life, I started collecting La Chuparrosa and reading scientific books like *Hummingbirds* by Crawford H. Greenewalt. The hummingbird flew into Matt's loft then exhausted itself looking for a way out. When it fell to the floor, he picked it up and sprinkled a drop of water on the back of its neck, since he'd heard that could revive tired hummingbirds. As the bird came to in the palm of his hand, he took it outside and watched it fly away.

The pharmacy was especially busy, but the man behind the counter recognized me and asked what I needed. He spoke English, which helped because my Spanish was limited.

"I don't know what I need, but I think I've been cursed," I told him. "I've had bad luck this summer."

"What kind of bad luck?" he asked.

"Physical, mostly. Pains all over. Bruises, sores, cuts. Do you think someone hates me? I try to be nice—"

"Perhaps someone is jealous of you," he interrupted. "You have something someone else wants, and they're bitter about it. Maybe a man."

"A man is jealous of me?"

"No, another woman," he said, leaning over the glass counter. "She has given you the Mal Ojo."

The pharmacist walked me around the store, filling my basket with oddities such as a blue candle shaped like a penis, perfume whose bottle bore a picture of a hand, and a charm baggie containing a red ribbon, a doll's eye, a fake lock of hair, and a tiny gold horseshoe. Finally, he gave me a talisman from behind the counter—a giant brown seed tied with red cord. "Ojo de venado," he said. "Wear this around your neck at all times."

Matt slept over after I showed him all the knick-knacks I'd been given to protect myself from Mal Ojo. The deer's eye necklace was gaudy but seemed more prescribed, and therefore more likely to help me than the hummingbird prayers, incense, books, and videos lying around. I burned the penis candle on the nightstand as we fell asleep, which I think worried him a little.

The following morning he asked, "How'd you sleep last night?"

"I dreamed I was sledding in the snow with hordes of baby penguins. They were so cute!"

"You're cute," he said.

Over coffee, I pulled a penguin book off the book-shelf. I read about the fossil remains of a five-foot penguin that weighed 250 pounds, and envisioned a penguin larger than myself. The chapter entitled "The Emperor's Domestic Life" documented a battle between two female emperor penguins who were hot for the same male. I imagined slapping some girl with my black, rubbery flipper. *I'd do it*, I mumbled. *I'd knock her over if I had to.*

"You'd do what?" Matt asked, as he sat down next to me on the couch.

"I'd slap any girl who tried to steal you, just like this penguin is doing here." I showed him the picture.

He smiled and pointed to the bottom of the page,

past the caption that noted how the *male ducks out of the way while the females glare at each other over his head.* There were two penguins—one tall, one short— touching bellies. The caption read: *The victorious female stands chest to chest with the hard-won prize and warbles the penguin love song.*

"There's us, after you knocked her out," he said.

"They're kissing," I said fondly, taking another gulp of coffee from my mug. "That is so insanely cute." It was then I realized I'd called penguins cute twice already that morning.

After the cuteness of the penguins waned, humming-birds were still on my mind, several of them in fact. My head was like a plastic raspberry-shaped nectar container; birds were poking their beaks at me from all directions, chipping away my skull to get the sweet gooey brain matter. I contemplated their mini machinery. I recalled that the *Calliphox amethystina*, one of the fastest, can beat its wings about eighty times per second! Hummingbirds are also the only birds that have a "reverse gear," which is why they can fly backwards. *They're like small power tools*, I thought.

After dinner that evening, we peeled the clothes off each other. But as we were getting into bed Matt said, "Take that weird seed necklace off."

I laid it next to the half-burned penis candle. As we were having sex, I pulled a muscle in my back.

"These injuries have to stop," I said, as he rubbed

Tiger Balm on my shoulder blade. "There's one more cure I haven't tried yet."

"What's that?" he asked.

"First, you have to hold an egg over me. Then we hide the egg under the bed for a few days. If the egg has a spot when we crack it open, that proves the Evil Eye's been absorbed into the egg."

The egg failed. I spent the next couple of days mentally running down the list of every female I'd interacted with in the past several years, but I couldn't remember pissing any of them off. My back was jacked. It was the climax of my pain, summer's low point. No female would have wished this—it was like delivering a baby nonstop, but from my spine like some alien birth. I thought of the meat counter in the grocery store and wondered if the times I looked at the fish too long might have enraged some ladies. I spent most of the season either inside the house with my boyfriend or outside on the porch where my rocking chair sat beneath the line of feeders I'd hung for hummingbirds.

Then I thought of Adele. She wouldn't have cursed me, though—she introduced me to my favorite beers, Humboldt Brewery's Nectar Ales series. Each ale depicts a green hummingbird on the label that sucks differently colored penstemon blooms. Red Nectar has red flowers, Gold Nectar has yellow flowers, Hemp Ale has pink flowers, and the Pale Ale has blue flowers. On each label there's a sunset behind the bird. One afternoon when we both lived up in the Redwoods she brought me a six-pack of Red Nectar, and told me how she skinny-dipped in the Eel River before she drank it because there was a river winding through the forest in the background on the label. She said the label was magic in an instructional, maplike sort of way—that you were supposed to interact with the environment according to what was on the label. So we went down to the river, found some flowers, and drank the beer at sunset. Hummingbirds buzzed around until it grew darker so bats could take over. At twilight, it was hard to distinguish bats from birds, but we noticed their flight patterns—the bats were clumsy and the hummingbirds darted around like geniuses.

So that's why I have hummingbird feeders on my porch. If I'm drinking a bottle of Nectar, I can watch them sip sweet juice along with me. I feel like a hummingbird when I drink that beer. It's not that I feel smarter, but rather sharp, pleasant, and relaxed. When I sit on the porch watching birds feast, I don't care about anything else.

A few mornings later, while Matt was taking a shower, I walked out onto the porch to inspect the plants and saw that all of the hummingbird feeders were empty. Six drained feeders were swinging from the porch beam. Usually, I noticed when they were low and refilled them with my specially sweet hummingbird nectar—three parts sugar, one part water—so the birds wouldn't go elsewhere to get juiced up. I'd had whole families raised on my feeders.

Two aggressive birds had been feuding over my feeders since spring—a male Rufous and a female Anna's—but this morning they were battling between two trees that framed the yard. As I stood there, their beaks grazed my head, and the sound of them whizzing by was scarier than bumblebees buzzing. Ducking to avoid being hit, I watched the birds fight, not making the J-flight patterns of a mating pair but flying directly at each other at top speed. I snatched the feeders off their nails and went inside to make the mixture.

Full feeders replaced, beer in hand, I sat in my rocker to wait for stoked chuparrosas to arrive. The bird on my beer label was the ideal happy bird. I wanted my birds to have that same passion for suckling juice. Adele came to mind and I remembered when she told me about skinny-dipping. She sat in this relaxed way, and I could see her lacy blue bra because her blouse was hanging open. Maybe she was putting the moves on me but I didn't react because I had a boyfriend. She was cute too—I always thought so. I don't think I can be friends with a woman if I'm not attracted to her in some way.

The female Anna's came first, her red-green feathers reflecting in the feeder's glass. She sipped on the red bubble, then moved to the red strawberry, drinking for minutes straight. Then I swear she looked down and gave me a dirty look. She also twitched her beak like a person would flip her hair or curl her upper lip in disgust, Billy Idol–style. I'd heard that male Rufouses were the meanest, but this

Anna's was fierce. She looked drunk, as if my feeders had finally provided her with the several shots of bird alcohol she'd wanted during withdrawals. I felt bad that I'd neglected to give the birds fresh juice for a few days; it never occurred to me that they'd develop a physical dependency on my high-octane humming-bird moonshine.

"I think I know who gave me the Mal Ojo!" I yelled inside the house.

I went into the bedroom, removed the penis can-dle from the nightstand, put it on a dish, and took it out to the porch, where it melted into a blue, waxy puddle. Then I placed it below the feeders in hopes of imprinting hummingbird tracks upon it. Back inside, I started slicing lemons to drop into a pitcher of sun tea. The knife slipped and cut through my fin-gernail. I sucked the blood off my finger, feeling happy to know where the pain came from. I thought of the bird, sucking her pain away.

START ME UP

When my mom and aunt were single, we lived in this bachelorette condo. I loved choreographing dances to the records they'd bring home—Fleetwood Mac, Genesis, Juice Newton. My aunt had a Doobie Brother-ish boyfriend, Bob, who had the face of a clown without makeup: it was roseate and overly happy in an unreadable way. He brought over some lobsters to cook one night after we'd already been pigging out on chocolate fondue with bread and cheese. I was thrilled to be eating chocolate for dinner and I wasn't initially opposed to the lobsters. Still, when I saw their rubber-banded claws, I felt a twinge of pity, and once my mom started to boil them, things got much worse.

There were four lobsters, two in each pot, and they exuded that gnarly ocean smell as soon as they hit hot water. For several minutes they cried in shrill tones—in a special lobster emergency pitch, I suppose, used to call fellow bottom feeders. It was this *EE-EE-EE* sound, as if they were trying to enunciate, "Don't cook me." It sounded like they were either emerging from the depths of hell or entering it.

"Please, mom, stop!" I yelled.

"They'll stop soon," my aunt answered. "We made the water real hot."

I didn't care. There was no justification for this abomination of a meal, especially compared to a sweet crock-pot full of melted Hershey's bars.

I had to block the cries from my ears like I was watching a horror movie. I pulled out the newly purchased Rolling Stones album, *Tattoo You*, and put on their hit song "Start Me Up." It all makes perfect sense to me now because it was the first time the power of rock really hit me. That song was the perfect backdrop for the Satanic party going on in the kitchen. I sat on the brown shag carpet in front of the speaker, following the catchy guitar riff that I adore to this day, and stared at the olive-green velvet patterns on the wallpaper. I have no recollection of the lobsters being consumed, but my mother says they were delectable and buttery. She claims that the cries I heard were imagined. How would an eight-year-old imagine the sound of death?

Shortly after that feast, my mom started dating this man who always brought me or my calico cat a present which I didn't want because it wasn't from my dad. He'd bring nail polish, catnip, key chains. He French-kissed my mom after each date—I always spied on them from behind the upstairs banister. My brother stayed in his bedroom, sleeping peacefully, and I wondered how he could rest knowing our mother was out there macking on a stranger. I questioned whether or not my mom was being forced to kiss this guy against her will, lured by the expensive dinners he bought her. Still, she didn't seem to fight when he reached his hairy hands behind her neck. I could see his face, eyes closed, swaying through the air like he was wasted on love. Their kisses were so lengthy that I had time to grab my cat and bring her back to pet her for the duration.

So how appalled was I when she and this same man got married and served lobster at their wedding dinner a few years later? I looked at that lobster on the white china plate and the Rolling Stones started playing in my head. My mom looked over at me and said, "You look pale, honey, try to eat," but there was no possibility of that. I started to feel nauseous and excused myself to go vomit in the banquet hall bathroom. My grandma held my hair back and said, "He's not so bad." She knew how messed up it was to be getting a stepfather. But since he wasn't mean, I had no real excuse to hate him.

In fact, a few years later when the *Beatles vs. Rolling Stones* debate had begun between my real father and I, my stepdad was the one who sided with me on the Rolling Stones' side. The two dads were making me decide which band reigned supreme, because apparently for true fans there was no middle ground. At first, when my real dad passed down his Beatles record collection to me, I'd freaked out on *The White Album* super hard. I sang the songs "Julia" and "I Will" in every shower because the length of time it took to sing those two songs in a row was a perfect amount of time to get clean. But then my stepdad gave me his first pressing of *Their Satanic Majesties Request*, persuading me to listen to it by hinting that all the Beatles' faces were hidden in the holographic cover. (I still haven't found Ringo.) When my real dad opted out and said he'd always liked The Who best anyway, I knew that my stepdad had won the battle, sort of. I mean, I still love the Beatles.

But the Rolling Stones rule. I love *Tattoo You*'s inner sleeve, showing a goat's hoof wearing a stiletto heel. This either means that women and animals are equal or that sexy women are demonic. Earlier Rolling Stones—from *Meet the Rolling Stones* to *Between the Buttons* with that jaunty song "Something Happened to Me Yesterday"—are great because Mick tries to sound cute but naughty. The more loaded-sounding *Goat's Head Soup* with "Angie" is okay, but Mick sounds constipated. When I play this album, I attune my ears to Charlie's epic drumming or to Ron's subtle bass lines. *Exile on Main Street* and *Some Girls* are both perfect. Every three years I have a Mick Jagger movie marathon, which begins and ends with *Rolling Stones Rock and Roll Circus*, featuring Brian Jones and Marianne Faithful, sick from just having aborted the baby that would have been Jagger's. Maybe she was nauseous like I was nauseous when I had to get a new parent—gaining and losing relatives must be similar. I watch her on film and think about how hard it would've been for her to do that scene, singing in a circus ring under the spotlight after such trauma. Mick must have a sadistic side—in *Cocksucker Blues*, a groupie sadly wonders aloud about what sperm she currently has inside her, Keith's or Mick's.

Speaking of sperm, here's the connection between Mick's sperm and the dread of acquiring a stepdad— having a new man in the house throws the balance off. I liked it when it was just my mom, my aunt (who was always visiting), and myself. My little brother counted, but he was too small to assert his male power. I sang Beatles songs in the shower because I wanted to channel my dad, my protector, while I was naked. Not to sound inbred, but I didn't want my stepdad coming in and dangling his penis around like a big guy. Nudity in the presence of your father is one thing, but nudity with a full-grown, musk-scented mystery man who's balling your mother is entirely different. It's not cool. He's the sperm spreader, the seed planter. And he's sowing his seeds in the wrong garden.

Lying in bed one night when I was seventeen—just before I moved out on my own—I had a conversation with Mick Jagger. I was thinking about how much I hated having this random man around the house, and I was getting really repulsed by the whole sperm thing. I'd been studying oocytes—reproduction and cellular biology—in science. Mick's voice came into my head, saying, in his British accent, "Sperm's not so bad, mate."

So I said, "Antoni van Leeuwenhoek discovered spermatozoa in 1679 during one of his research sessions wherein he placed semen under his self-made microscopes." I was totally nerdified. "Leeuwenhoek claimed that he got his sperm samples 'not by sinfully defiling himself, but as a natural consequence of conjugal coitus.'"[1]

Jagger laughed. "Yeah, right." Then he asked, "What else did this sick bloke do?"

"He dissected animals' genital organs," I said. "For example, he cut the testicles off a rabbit so he could see how many sperm were inside it."

"And what is this I hear about your not liking lobster meat, young lady?" Jagger asked. "I eat it constantly because it makes me horny."

[1] "Leeuwenhoek's Perception of Spermatozoa," http://zygote.swarthmore.edu/fert1a.html

THE TIDE OF MY MOUNTING SYMPATHY

> *But get thee back, my soul is too much charg'd*
> *With Blood of thine already.*
> —Macbeth, Act V sc. 7

My friend Karen walks in, out of breath and wearing one shoe.

"Your fucking friend just attacked me," she says.

She was in my basement music room so no one heard her yelling through the egg-crate covered walls. I'm hosting a Hawaiian-themed party. Ukuleles were blaring until I turned them down to hear her out. Apparently, Karen was playing guitar when John flipped the light switch off, grabbed her leg, and yanked off her sandal, which was strapped around her ankle. Her ankle's turning purple!

"What's wrong with him?" she asks.

"Why did he want your shoe?" I ask.

"He tried to rub my calf. Then I started yelling

and he wouldn't let me leave," she says.

We can hear someone hurling in the bathroom. I feel so ashamed it's like I stole the shoe. Then Charlie, a man I barely know, tells us he's going downstairs to "throw the creep out." That creep used to be my friend. I didn't invite him tonight, but he heard about it somehow and came anyway. Charlie brings John through the kitchen, where I'm watching Karen rub her ankle.

"You have to leave," I say to him.

"What did I do?" he asks.

"You attacked Karen," I say. "Get out. Don't come back."

Karen stands behind me. "Give me my shoe," she says. John pulls it from the back of his pants. What a freak.

John walks down the street, cussing the whole way. My house is on Macbeth Street. That's the main reason I moved in. *Macbeth* is my favorite Shakespeare play. I attribute violent outbreaks to the street name. I'm careful to eliminate weapon-like items from my list of belongings because one day I might go crazy and start chopping people up like in the Polanski film. I would've made *Macbeth* a gorefest too if my wife had just been stabbed to death by Mansons.

One time, John grabbed me and tried to kiss me. Another time, he stole my camera that had pictures of my girlfriends and me in bathing suits. At my old house, he used to sit on my porch waiting for me to come out. Every couple hours I'd crack the door open and ask him to leave. "I don't want to talk to you," I'd say. He'd sweat, telling me he had to see me. When I asked him why, he'd mumble something about my socks, or say, "Hey, I like those jeans you're wearing," and I'd shut the door in his face. He kept escaping from the mental hospital. He had taken too much acid and started stalking girls during his first semester of college. He'd hang around the dorms even after being expelled, following girls to class then waiting outside their classrooms. I felt sorry for him; he had restraining orders against him, and doctors said he was schizophrenic. I never called the police when he bothered me. He was tripping out on female beauty. I wasn't flattered, but I suppose I was glad he didn't think I was repulsive. He didn't seem dangerous, just fetishistic. He'd show up now and then, and I'd wonder how he got my phone number or address.

I read werewolf books to comprehend how a person can be so attracted to someone that he wants to devour them. Lycorexia is a canine desire that manifests in humans as a need to stuff oneself with human flesh. But werewolves crave putrid meat. John wants live women. Sometimes I imagine what he would do to me if I let him trip out all the way. Would he eat me? He's hairy. I think he would bite. The time he tried to kiss me, he pulled my head toward his mouth and clumsily pressed my lips hard against his teeth, as if I were a ripe peach he was biting into. His hand clutched the back of my head. To gain control, I had to peel his hand off with both of mine. Are his teeth sharp? Does he get vicious at night? Does he howl? Does he have two personalities?

The next morning, we wake up from our drunken stupors. The house reeks of piss because someone took a leak on the couch. Karen and I drag the cushions out to the curb, then the frame. I'll get a new sofa. That one was only $25 at the thrift store. There are seven people who never made it home. One guy puts coffee on, and Karen and I talk about John some more.

"You should stay away from him," she says.

"I try, but he finds me," I say. "He's not going to hurt anyone, he's just gross."

"What if you're alone though?" she asks. "He's weird."

"Barf Man was weird," I say.

Barf Man was Joshua, another grody guy who used to bug me. I literally had to move across the state to get rid of him. He'd give girls heroin if they'd never used it so they would get high and barf. Once you got used to getting high, he'd lose interest because you weren't barfing enough for him to get off. He was six feet tall, had long black hair down to his butt, and always wore a shiny black trenchcoat and hat. He had a Glock collection.

"Want to see my new gun?" he asked me.

"Sure," I said.

We were alone in my dorm room. It was my

sophomore year of college, about 2 a.m. I had a history test the next day, but I decided I'd rather look at a weird man's gun than study Mesopotamia. Joshua put a bundle on my bed and unwrapped his Glock, a handgun of some sort. I don't know about guns, except that some are ugly and some are elegant. This one was slender, had a comfortable handle, and looked like a gun James Bond would use.

"It's pretty," I said.

"Let's go to the beach," he said. He looked down at the floor, sad and resolved. I had no idea what he was sad about.

We drove an hour out to the beach, over windy roads through farmland. He told me he was bringing his loaded gun to protect us. We parked his beat-up old Volvo station wagon, smoked some heroin, and then he asked me to climb into the back end with him. I realized maybe he had been sad back in my room because he thought he was going to kill me. I figured it was better to make out with him than to die. He was a moody dude. He'd come into my room sometimes and start bawling, crying so hard he couldn't even tell me what was wrong.

When he tried to roll on top of me, I had to think of something quick. I told him I felt sick. He perked up and grew sympathetic, like I was his baby bird and he was going to feed me a worm. He walked me to the end of the pier where I bent over and made myself puke into the water. That's the only time I've been able to barf on command. My legs felt rubbery, and Joshua was clearly into this. He stooped beside me, looking up through my legs at my spewing mouth.

"Sit down. I'll hold your hair back," he said.

I got down on my knees. He pulled my hair back in this romantic way, kind of brushing it with his fingers and rubbing the side of my face. Then he leaned over my shoulder so he could see me barf.

"Don't watch," I said.

"Don't be embarrassed," he said. "I know how you feel."

Whatever, freak, I thought. The word *freak* played repeatedly in my head. *Freakiest scene ever. What a total freak. I am such a freak for barfing off a pier for some freakish man who has a loaded gun in his pocket. I'm tired of freaks. Get away, freak. What a freakin' mess. This is freaky. What a fucking freak. Freaky, man. I can't even deal with this freak.*

"I finished barfing and he drove me home," I tell Karen.

"Did you talk to him after that?" she asks.

"A little, until one night I caught him helping my roommate barf into our toilet," I say.

Everyone has their favorite body parts. I like shoulders, arms, and hands. Karen likes feet. She gets custom shoes made: ones that imitate that high 1940s heel on those round-toed pumps. Joshua liked seeing mouths make wrong shapes. Werewolves like hair. They like hairy women because they know hair's sexual potential. Hair equals sex for werewolves. Pictures of werewolves often show women fallen backwards in the wolf's arms. The unconscious woman's hair dangles down, her mouth open. Sometimes her face is shown. Sometimes her hair covers it. I prefer it when the girl's awake and you can compare her look of terror to the wolf's rage and hunger. I understand why the wolf's so into that. He likes to dominate. Barf turns wolves on too, I'm sure. When my dog was a puppy, he used to lick up my cat's barf until I taught him not to. He stops to smell barf when we're walking, and I yank on his leash to keep him moving. He likes getting his leash yanked while he smells barf. Just kidding! Even my dog isn't as sick as the freaks who pester me.

John's in the hospital again. He calls from the pay phone asking me to come visit. I decide to go because I know no one else will. Plus, he wants cigarettes. I feel so bad for people who are locked up and can't smoke. I take cigarettes to both friends and ex-friends. I make exceptions. I feel bad enough for John because his main pleasure happens to be one that bothers other people. I try so hard to find pleasures I can keep to myself. Even things you do alone, like getting drunk, can rub people the wrong way. It's just a matter of how far you take it.

John's hospital room is the same one another friend of mine stayed in. It's so fucked. The room is too tiny. I ask John to walk out into the hall with me, but he won't get off the bed. He keeps asking me to sit down. I tell him I'd rather stand. Finally, I just sit so he'll talk about other things. We stare at the walls together, and I wonder what pills he's taking. He's still obsessing over me, but he's not shouting or cussing. He blinks a lot, like his eyes are dried out. He reaches over and puts his hand on my leg.

"Don't," I say.

He takes his hand away. His meds are working. Before, it was like he was deaf. He's still freaking out, but not in such an oblivious way. I hate this hospital.

"How long do you have to be in here?" I ask.

His eyes open wide. "What do you want from me?" he asks.

"Nothing, I just came to give you smokes and say hi."

"Why are you asking me so many questions?" he asks.

"I only asked one," I say. It feels so great that we're having a real conversation, a linear one with Q & A. I like arguing when the argument makes sense.

"Are you allowed to go outside?" I ask.

"Hey, I like your tits," he says. He looks sadly at the floor, already knowing what will happen next.

FACES

I. Mosquito Face

My face is not exactly like two dogs humping, but it's just as fascinating and embarrassing. Last week it was devoured by mosquitoes when my brother and I hiked through dry grass and blue oak forest to a lake. Since there was no moon, it was sort of like climbing Mt. Everest. When we finally stumbled onto the shore, we imagined the animals protesting our visit were geese, cows, bullfrogs, or some combination thereof. I thought it was a goose-cow-frog. My brother thought it was an angry bull. We sat down and looked into the darkness at the silhouettes of the "mighty oaks," as they're called in my book, *Oaks of California*. Then we heard a car screech and slam into something down below.

Some frenetic Northern Lights appeared, pink

behind the trees. The glow was accompanied by the sound of electricity escaped into the air, snapping noises generated from fallen power lines that were whipping the earth and cracking back upwards. The noise of the car getting doused with current, a series of erratic revs followed by desperate honks from a misfiring horn, came after the snaps. He'd plugged himself into the town's main power box. All the local light faded and joined us in blackness. Then the sirens started. We walked down the hill and smoked some more pot.

This combination of noises—animals cooing, croaking, chirping, and hopping, the car's sputtering engine amidst police and ambulance sirens, and power lines leaking sparks and crackling almost like metal popcorn—kept us mesmerized for at least an hour, during which I acquired fifty bites. Seven of them are on my face.

II. Lizard Face

Steve Miller Band was singing, *Big ol' jet airliner, carry me to my home*, at the Silver Bowl in Las Vegas. Harley-Davidson biker dudes were getting their T-shirts all wet under these pierced hoses that were suspended around the stadium. All the men had long, stringy hair, and their beer bellies looked like wobbly piles of dung stuck onto their torsos. I had on green leather Birkenstocks. I pushed into the mist, fighting my way through this sea of bellies to cool off in the August heat. My feet turned green from the bleeding sandals, and I felt slimy like a lizard.

That's why when I saw my face in the reflection of my friend's Zippo later that evening, I thought I'd become some mutant lizard human. I stuck out my tongue, watched for a passing fly, and snapped it back. My face was covered in scales and the skin was pale olive-green. My cheekbones had sunk so deep I had a long alligator snout. I felt prehistoric. I was like a fossil of my once reptilian self. I remembered lying on rocks to let my cold blood thaw. My face was full of crevices and dark, shadowy wrinkles, and I knew at that moment, staring into the mystical Zippo, that it was time to chill out and smoke a cigarette.

III. No Face

In northern Idaho, along the fork of the three main rivers that run through the state—the Lochsa, Salmon, and Snake—I rode my horse Rainbow through berry bushes and nettles. I guess horses are immune to stinging nettles because she didn't complain. I gave her extra foods like carrot sticks, leaves, and trail mix. Every day at sunset, I stopped to camp beside the river. I put the Jethro Tull tape into my Walkman, listened to Ian Anderson's flute trips, and imagined him in medieval, lace-up leather boots. I'd stand like he stood on stage, balancing on one leg, the other in a V with foot propped against calf, still covered by brown leather. The boots came up to his knees, so rad, stylish but practical. Ian was dorky like a father, not sexy. I took tips from him because his music alternated between calm and tempestuous— I figured I could travel just by listening.

Several days passed before I saw myself in a mirror. Those were great days. I figured Ian Anderson didn't look in mirrors as he played the flute. When I did finally see myself, posing in the Ian Anderson flamingo stance in a gas station mirror, I felt ridiculous. My hair looked like I'd undergone shock treatment. I patted it down with wet hands, thinking, *I've been living in a dork palace.* After that, I avoided mirrors. I took them off all the walls.

My other mirror-phobic period began the night a Snowy White Owl flew in front of my windshield. I was driving to a field outside Eureka. Llamas lived on this ranch, and I wanted to check them out. It was 3 a.m. Owls were always flying around and dodging cars up there. I don't know why it was such an omen, but at the time, I was a vampire and the owl was my death animal, the animal I knew I'd see before dying completely. Your body can die and your soul will live on, but if you see your death animal it means that when you die, you will die both physically and spiritually forever. Therefore, I believed that although I was immortal in my vampire status, the owl symbolized imminent termination of all aspects of my soul, evil and non-evil.

In the days following this experience, all I could drink was orange juice because the sweet, sour, pulpy taste reminded me of the very center of life, the core kindness of all living beings, the sphere of the sun and the heat generated from within. I drank lots of juice, and the sugar made me a little neurotic.

I feared the mirror and covered it. For, you see, vampires can see their reflections, and if I'd failed to see mine, that would have meant I was . . .

IV. Jerky Face

A Chinese man told me my face looked like burnt beef. What did he mean by that? Did he mean to say beautiful apple? Did he mean smooth, brown, supple? When you pull it apart, it's a compliment: the burntness being an evenly tanned and healthily cooked face, and the beef being the delicious flesh of the animal kingdom. I said thank you, and walked away.

I admit at times my face is leathery, but I am no leatherfaced serial killer. At times I seem Mexican, because I tan easily. Kids tell me I look Latino, but I'm not. "You must eat beans," they say, and while I love beans, that doesn't make me Mexican. Plus, practically everyone on this planet loves beans.

When people are hungry, they see food in your face. The cartoons are true: You do turn into a giant chicken drumstick or steaming ham. I'm surprised my friends haven't eaten me. But if they do, remember this story, find my bones picked apart and licked clean, gather my cartilage into a gelatinous pile, then bury me so my dog can dig me up and chew on me until I'm splintered all throughout my garden of calendula.

GET COMFORTABLE

If you want comfort you should give up learning;
If you desire to acquire learning you should abandon comfort.
How can a person who wants comfort acquire learning?
And how can a person enjoy comfort who wants to learn?
—Sanskrit proverb

I. Dream Job

I'd like to own a yacht, a big-ass Boston Whaler on which DJs spin reggae and people smoke spliffs. On my perfect boat, smoke is sweet and wafts off into clouds for dolphins to enjoy, and girls in bikinis dive off the rail to swim with them. It's kind of like a pimped-out rap video boat, but there are no sleazy macho men or catty ho's. No butt-pinching or gold chains. Visitors would grow swarthy with rum, stumbling around in a jolly trance. I'd have a monkey as host in a striped T-shirt, a miniature three-corner hat, and an eye patch. There'd be a flag with skull and crossbones on the red, gold, and green.

"You should think of a backup plan," my friend Heidi tells me when I call her in Maui, where she lives. "There are lots of people with boats here," she says. "They all get stoned, but not many of them make a living doing it."

"I need a job where I can exercise," I say. "I'm too fat to fit into my bathing suit. You swam with the dolphins, right?"

"Yeah. Maybe you should work at Club Med."

"I'm not going to smoke out all those rich house-wives," I reply. "On the other hand, they could afford to buy me pot."

"Having rich friends is key," she says.

There's something evil about a world in which I can think of a hundred jobs I'd like, and none of them will support me. Puppy rancher, wild mush-room collector, designer of fantasy postal stamps, incense critic. I'd like to run a sticker museum, where I'd curate shows: *The History of Scratch and Sniffs*, or *Great Designs: Stars and Rainbows*. But who would come?

When I was little my favorite book was *Charlotte's Web* because Charlotte made a brilliant career for herself, one that nobody else could have helped her with. She benefited everyone, especially Wilbur, through her craft and language. Wilbur, though, made a career of being cute. I got so pissed off when Wilbur got buttermilk baths instead of Charlotte. Wilbur got credit for being Zuckerman's Famous Pig when it was Charlotte who should've been winning ribbons at the fair. Charlotte was the smart one, and all she did was die up in the rafters after laying a thousand eggs. I'm still not convinced that Wilbur's friendship with Charlotte's offspring constitutes a happy ending, because it only shows hard work as paying off if you consider having children a payoff. The saying, *Creativity is its own reward*, is conditional.

II. Firm Mattress

Walking the switchback trail through tanoak forest—my backpack on, boyfriend behind me—makes me feel like an elf leading a march for peace. Squirrels line up on the red, curly branches that weave themselves together into insane tree baskets. I can barely see the sky. Leaves crunch under my feet, but softly like the sound of the wind, all of which plays further into the squirrel fantasy Matt and I are elaborating. We imagine that only squirrels populate the world. They permit us, elves, to pass through their territory because elves are similar to squirrels. (They both have pointy ears and can walk stealthily.) We get so tired that we stop to lie at the base of a large madrone tree to communicate with all the living creatures in it. The ants, squirrels, tit wrens, robins, a crow, worms, and beetles share their space with us. Matt uses his elfin X-ray vision to study the tree-half that's underground, and I commit to everything from the trunk up.

While Matt's slumped into an unnatural position (as if he's just been punched) communing with roots and worms, I stretch out on our blanket and gaze upwards to observe the pattern the tree grows in: a seemingly chaotic but absolutely geometric spiral. Each time a branch springs out from a larger one, it curves clockwise to avoid collisions. And the squirrels that skitter around and around these branches are doing the same thing, navigating clockwise as they carry their stashes from ground to hole. The wood is shiny and smooth against the squirrels' brushed coats. I'd always thought squirrels had a superb sheen until I compare them to the gloss of this tree.

The point is: squirrels are doing everything in their power to make decent homes for themselves, and since their world is so screwy, this reminds me of how hard it is to exist. *Is it really worth it?* I wonder. But the squirrels inspire me. They don't sit around trying to decide if life's worth it. For them, nothing beats eating acorns in a warm, dry bed.

"I really want to get a comfortable bed," I say. "Squirrels have comfortable beds."

"Then why shouldn't we?" Matt asks.

III. Delectable Food

On special occasions, we drink flutes of champagne and Matt fixes roast pork. He slathers the flesh with mint and garlic, and ties string around it to make it juicier. We associate pork with luxury because it makes the house smell rich. The dog perks up at the chance that this may be the day he scores big time. Pork makes me feel like I'm living large.

We're celebrating the success of Matt's newest

painting. It's as long as a Honda, and as tall as our ceiling. Red-barked trees, squirrels, and naked women cover the canvas.

We discuss how great the painting is while chewing meat.

"I love these crusty bits," I say.

"I saved them for you."

He's a master chef. I'd be bony if he didn't feed me so well. Before I met Matt, I survived on lima beans, fruit leathers, and cream of wheat.

I tell him about the time my brother and I tried to scrape together a couple of bucks to buy ice cream. It was like the Great Depression.

"Those days are over," Matt says. I look down at my plate of pork accompanied by mustard greens, saffron-and-turmeric rice, and tomato salad. There will be tons of leftovers. Tomorrow it'll be easy for me to make myself lunch.

The next day I come home from work and find Matt doubled over on the couch (again as if he's been punched). He blames it on the pork, but I feel fine. I run out to get him ginger ale and saltines. When I get back he confesses that after I'd gone to work, he'd eaten pork for breakfast.

"There's nothing wrong with pork for breakfast," I say. "People eat bacon."

"But I finished the whole thing," he says. "I ate it straight out of the baking dish. It was like ten servings."

"I know," I say. "It tasted so good."

"I barfed hard," he says.

I had assumed as much.

"Pork fat chunks were floating in the toilet," he says. "It looked like boba."

Boba are translucent tapioca balls that come in Vietnamese drinks.

"Shut *up*," I say.

"I just ate a huge pile of lard, basically."

He's like decadent old King Louis, I think, *cooking up his maid's canary and making her watch him eat it*. I love feeling like the maid.

IV. Equal Union

I've been reading passages from the *Kama Sutra* before bed every night so I can mentally prepare myself for stress the next day. (I'll admit I read it for sexual advice too.) The section called *Ratavasthapana Prakarana* applies not only to the male/female union but also to unions of all sorts, both human and animal. Its animalistic mix-and-match metaphors apply to sex as well as attitude adjustment for dealing with weirdos. Sometimes as I'm waiting in line or sitting in traffic I see a guy bossing his girlfriend around and think, *Horse and deer, not the best*.

When I first read it, I used to dream about jungle orgies: lions humping wildebeests and boa constrictors riding panthers.

"Man is divided into three classes—*shaksa*, the hare; *vrisha*, the bull; and *ashwa*, the horse—according to the size of his *lingam*, or phallus. A woman too, according to the depth of her *yoni*, vagina, is either a *mrigi*, female deer; *vadava*, a mare; or a *hastini*, female elephant.

"There are three equal unions between persons of corresponding dimensions and six unequal unions when the dimensions do not correspond, or nine kinds of union in all. In unequal unions, when the male exceeds the female in point of size, his union with a woman immediately next to him in size is called a high union and it is of two kinds, while his union with a woman most remote from his size is called the higher union and is of one kind only. When the female exceeds the male in point of size, her union with a man immediately next to her in size is called low union and is of two kinds, while her union with a man farthest from her in size is called the lower union and is of one kind only.

Equal

Male	Female
Hare	Deer
Bull	Mare
Horse	Elephant

Unequal

Male	Female
Hare	Mare
Hare	Elephant
Bull	Deer
Bull	Elephant
Horse	Deer
Horse	Mare

"In other words, the horse and the mare, and the bull and the deer, form the high union; while the horse and the deer form the highest union. On the female side, the elephant and the bull, and the mare and the hare, form low unions; while the elephant and the hare form the lowest unions.

"There are then nine kinds of unions according to dimensions. Equal unions are the best; the highest and the lowest are the worst. The rest are middling, and among them high unions are considered better than low, for in a high union, the male can satisfy his own passion without hurting the female; in a low union, it is difficult for a female to be satisfied in any manner."

V. Favorite Song

If we can't sleep, Matt puts on music. I like how he takes charge of the situation instead of lying there brooding all night like I do. The desire to hear music may or may not be as primal a need as food, sleep, or sex, but listening to music is necessary.

The days of wine and roses
Are distant days to me

That's Donovan singing my favorite song of his, "Writer in the Sun," which he composed in 1966 during a trip to Greece. Even though the words are sad, the melody is relaxing and it has this timeless quality—it makes you feel that any situation is endurable because it's fleeting. I play the song in my head at work when I feel like quitting. Donovan strums the guitar steadily as if he's marching in a funeral procession.

The magazine girl poses
On my glossy paper aeroplane
Too many years I spent in the city
Playing with Mr. Loss and Gain

He reminds me to spend time outdoors contemplating what irritates me so that I can let it go. Last night I was out for drinks with some girlfriends talking about how people are always trying to beat each other out for Creative Person Of The Century. But then I can't just bail for paradise like my friend who swims with dolphins. I envy people who can enjoy themselves.

I bathe in the sun of the morning
Lemon circles swim in the tea
Fishing for time with a wishing line
And throwing it back in the sea

Donovan saw time changing and turning back in on itself. The belief that things happen for a reason is implied in his sound. It's a calming idea, one that I like to think is true. But why has it taken me so long to get comfortable?

SINNERS

Two Band-Aids, crisscrossed like a beige plus sign, block the peephole on my grandma's front door. To the right, a bronze crucifix doubly protects her from the dangers outside. She recently told me a cougar was stalking her from the roof. When someone knocks she warns me that it might be the neighbor who steals her trash.

"Who cares if someone steals your trash?" I ask. I turn the doorknob.

"It's my trash, I don't want anyone looking at it," she whispers.

Cruise brochures and health insurance papers describe the Twilight Years—the phase when you're too old to work but too young to drop dead—as potentially the best years of your life. Old people can finally reap the benefits of what they've sown—children, retirement pensions, social security, friendships—unless they're like my grandma, a friendless money squanderer whose children can't stand her. She used to be tactful and friendly, but that façade wore away years ago, morphing into paranoia mixed with suicidal comments.

"I'm so tired of living," she sighs over the phone.

"Come on, it's not that bad. You have like twenty years left. Why don't you go to church, or volunteer somewhere?"

"I'm too old to go to church," she complains.

My grandma's an Evangelist who watches ladies with pancake makeup and blue hair preach about Jesus. She donates to TBN, so sales representatives fill her answering machine with messages. I guess she likes the social interaction. When someone faints on stage during Sunday worship, claiming to be cured, she's really touched. Her version of Faith is an understanding that as long as she only goes outside to check the mailbox, God will continue to deliver Social Security checks.

My mom and I are packing up Grandma's belongings because she's moving into a nursing home. Mom says she's not officially senile, but she can't live alone anymore. The apartment smells fishy. The old blue carpet is crunchy with dried crumbs of canned cat food. Years of grease are smeared on the stovetop. The oven is a closet full of pots and pans she couldn't wash. I clear out the kitchen cabinets, filling trash bags with Tupperware and old plastic forks and spoons. There are about 400 ketchup packets in the drawer by the sink.

Grandma's in the bedroom instructing my mom what to pack or throw away. Every few minutes she calls to me, "You haven't thrown anything away, have you?"

"I'm just boxing stuff," I yell back as I tie up two more trash bags. I put a few things in open boxes to prove I didn't chuck everything.

Back in the bedroom, there's a pile of old bras that Mom wants to toss out. Grandma's so mad she's crying.

"These are my things, why are you telling me what to do with them?"

"These bras are from the '60s. I'll get you new ones," Mom says.

The only way to get packed is to put her in another room. I bring her out to her beloved armchair.

"Stay out of this," she tells me.

Mom and I unclog a closet while Grandma sorts magazines in the living room. I find a jewelry box. It's full of rhinestone brooches, gold-plated clip-on earrings, with some fine things mixed in—a strand of pearls, lapis lazuli bracelet, small diamond pendant, and two tarnished rings.

"That's my great-grandfather's old ring," my mom says. "I always wanted it."

"What's this one?" I ask, attracted to the ruby.

"That was your great-grandmother's," Mom says.

"You should have it," she adds, under her breath as if it's an illegal thought.

"You take that one," I say. We're excited to have real family heirlooms. They're rare in our family. We slide the rings into our purses.

"What are you two doing in there?" Grandma calls, and I take the jewelry box out to show her.

"Here's your jewelry. I'm putting it in your carry-on."

"You should never have touched that! It's none of your business." She grabs the box and rummages through to see what's missing.

"We're here to help, and you accuse us of thievery. That's it!" I yell, heading outside to smoke a cigarette. But first I pull the ring out of my purse and put it on so she can see. She's too busy looking into the box to notice.

"Just get out," she calls after me. "I'm sorry you have such a bitch for a mother."

I have absolutely no faith that some god will redeem my grandma for her ill manners, but at the same time, I don't think she'll burn in hell. I do believe I have a right to inherit some piece of history, some birthright. When you're born, you grow up having faith in the people who raise you, even if they're crabby and psycho. I figure you should get some proof you belong to them, like a ring, or a few photos. It's strange how confessional and indignant one can become while gazing into a gemstone's facets.

* * *

A few weeks after my grandma moves away, I eat Chinese food at a Szechwan restaurant in Chinatown and get a fortune cookie: *Faith is a beautiful twilight that enhances every object.* I think about twilight while I crunch on a chewy mushroom called Cloud-Ears. Out the window, streetlights become more and more glowey and reflective, and cars begin to flip on their headlights.

The Peking ducks hanging in a window across the street grow fiery and luminescent as the heat lamps behind them become orange spotlights in the darkness. Ordering my next drink, I think of all the drinks mixed to look like twilight: Tequila Sunrise, Singapore Sling, Blue Dragon (which uses blue curaçao as its bottom layer), Cape Cod, Long Island Iced Tea. Sunset drinks mimic their environment, which is profound considering they're only beverages.

Twilight is the most beautiful time because you have only darkness to compare it to. Twilight precedes death. Twilight, when things are visually reversed, is the ideal time to exhibit faith in something. Twilight is a time to stop being skeptical. I guess this Transcendentalist view allows for the worship of natural wonders. It beats praying with some blue-haired lady on TV. Once a day you have faith that the universe isn't totally evil, that there are things beyond your control, and you might as well stop to appreciate them.

I hope I can appreciate my grandma before she dies.

* * *

After I get the fortune cookie, I call my mom on the phone and ask why Grandma is such an evil bitch.

"Don't call her that," Mom says.

"She called you a bitch," I say.

"She's had a hard life," Mom begins. I've heard Grandma's Louisiana swamp stories before, so I'm not in the mood to rehash how she couldn't even afford toilet paper. I don't want to hear about how her family used to take day trips to go see the whippin' posts at the port where the slave ships used to dock. That's what Grandma used to tell me—but then I remember that this ring I'm wearing belonged to one of those backwater people, and I feel ashamed.

"Are we white trash for stealing the rings?" I ask, hoping she'll say, *Yes, we are going to rot underground for this one*, just so I can feel honest.

"No. That ring is yours. Grandma would want you to have it. I could call her right now, tell her you have it, and she'd be thrilled." Mom may be right, but I think she's wrong. Grandma would hate me.

"Maybe we should call her and confess." Then I read Mom the fortune, and mention that Grandma's in her twilight years. "She doesn't have much faith in us."

"Neither do you," Mom says. I breathe hot air on my ruby ring and polish it on my jeans before changing the subject.

My dream after the fortune cookie, after the phone conversation about who's evil and who's white trash, involves a ghost murderer floating beside me as I row through mandrake roots and Spanish moss in a skinny, winding canal. The air smells dank like rotten Band-Aids, plasticine and poisonous. The killer leads me to his lair and chops me up. Fingers come off one by one. I lie face down in red, bloody water. My extremities waft off to shore where baby gators can fight over them.

I see creatures swimming beneath me. The water's colors are stratified like a twilight sky: red, orange, pink, green, blue, black. Crabs crawl by. Long eels slither across my peripheral vision. Fish, crawdads, and mosquito larvae hook back and forth, back and forth. But I don't care, because I'm only parts now.

A manatee swims up close and sniffs me with his big, whiskered snout. His skin is beautiful and gray. My eyes open wider to see him clearly, and he gives me a brush with his paw. He's my first friend in the afterlife, a savior much more appealing than any god. No, he doesn't represent my grandma, the murderer does. I think of sailors mistaking sea cows for mermaids after long, lonely voyages at sea. Sea cows are like underwater angels, especially with their feathery flippers. I wake up wondering, *Is he my mom, my dog, a cigarette, some beer, a fortune in a cookie, pretty mixed drinks, the darkening sky, Chinatown, or the ring?*

It's true. I have no faith in us. I stole a family heirloom. I drank beer and smoked while I wore it. My mom convinced me to do it. When I think of Grandma, I think of a woman possessed by the devil. I picture her head twirling 360° over and over on her shoulders. Then I picture myself possessed by a demon I don't even theoretically believe in. I sinned. The manatee saved me. We're all sinners, my idiotic swamp relatives too.

ANIMAL PARTY

I used to play a lot of Burgertime. I was living by myself in the Mojave Desert, and coyotes had just eaten my cat. Burgertime is a Nintendo game where the player is Chef Pepper, best burger-maker in the world. Chef Pepper positions buns so that lettuce, tomatoes, and yellow cheese will fall onto them from outer space. Since the game design is primitive, the ingredients are chunky and squared and the colors are flat. The lettuce doesn't have the real thing's multiple shades of green. The buns are solid brown, and their rounded edges look zigzaggy, as if they're cross-stitched. Since Burgertime is my favorite video game, I sometimes think I should embroider a quilt covered with hamburgers and Chef Pepper's arch villains: Mr. Hot Dog, Mr. Pickle, and Mr. Egg. Quilts are also useful weapons in the fight against loneliness.

At first it didn't seem like I'd be lonely in the desert, what with so many critters around. The day I moved in, I walked barefoot on the patio and got stung by red ants. The ants were the color of my burgundy toenail polish. If I stood still, they circled my feet and prepared to ascend my ankles. The colony was so extensive that I felt like I should've petitioned their queen for the right to live there.

Then a fruit bat moved in. He flew in the window one night while I sat on my couch in the dark watching thunderstorms in the distance. The lightning cracked, making neon hairline-fractures in the sky, only to reassemble in clouds that glowed on and off like a lightbulb with an old filament. The bat flew up to my ceiling and perched upside down. When I turned on the light to see its reflective nocturnal eyes, it looked back in a gentle way that I interpreted as happiness to see me. The bat lived there for two weeks, munching on insects in the rafters.

At one point a praying mantis lived inside my curtain folds. It started out tan, an inch long, then grew three inches while turning bright green. It would crawl out of the curtain to perch in front of me when I stood at the sink washing dishes. It seemed like my mantis loved me, or at least was curious. In desolate regions, animals and humans have to band together for company and social interaction, I guess.

The bat didn't eat the mantis.

I moved to the desert to escape the noise and crap in

Los Angeles. L.A.'s air felt gunky on my skin. Just walking outside I'd acquire greasy layers. I washed my face three or four times a day. Four hounds next door started barking at dawn every morning. The city felt claustrophobic and dingy, even at night when I was most alive. I couldn't see stars. I'd sit at my desk spying through binoculars into other people's houses. Even then, I only saw TVs flickering—no naked woman dancing, no stoner getting high. Everyone was so boring. Worst of all, I hated driving the grids; it made me feel stupid, like a termite. All the daily plugging away in the car, on the phone, on the computer, in the kitchen, shopping, getting dressed, talking, thinking, behaving, and controlling amounted to nothing more than survival, something that a termite does so easily with no financial security or brains.

It wasn't fair: all the responsibilities, all the years of moral preparation and schooling, for no more accomplishment (a rented house, decent meals) than that of an insect. You think humans are superior, but they're really not—think of all the amazing feats termites can pull off that we can't: chewing and digesting wood, carrying things hundreds of times their weight, building massive muddy towers and secure tunnel systems, communicating telepathically without language. Being human is a gyp.

So when my first cat was fatally hit by a car, I decided to move where animals lived more naturally, where the species intermingled, where I could feel more like an animal. But then my second cat died.

* * *

The only official party I hosted in the desert was a Burgertime Party. About eight friends drove out from the city to spend the night. They were old friends whom I hadn't seen in months. They'd been offended when I moved away, as if I were snubbing them for being dull. At the time, I was. But after a year of solitudinous living, I was tired of hosting animal parties, during which I'd down a couple bottles of red wine while searching every room and porch for other living things—kangaroo rats, moths, lizards, scorpions. Here's a typical animal party:

1. Snoop through the vegetable bin in the refrigerator for leafy greens. Tear half a leaf off something.
2. Hunt the pantry for seeds, sunflower or sesame, for instance, and put some in a cup.
3. Look for something to feed the snacks to. If nothing reveals itself, go visit the black widow in her web on the back porch, leaving a small food pile beneath her. Do not hand feed.

Nights became so nonverbal.

So at the video game event we sat in a tendril-like arc around the TV screen with cords connecting us to the electronics. The Middle Eastern–inflected Burgertime theme song made us feel like we were surrounded by belly dancers in some exotic, smoky nightclub. I tried to remember how to make conversation.

"Put the cheese down before you sprinkle pepper

on the egg. That's the only way you'll have time to finish the level," I told my friend Belinda.

"I'm so bad at these games!" she yelled, and threw down the controller.

Jordan, a more serious video game player, told me, "You must've mastered this thing by now. You have so much time to play."

"No," I said. "I'm pathetic. Even if I played twenty-four hours a day, I couldn't win. The pickle kicks my ass every time." This confession made me somber again, since I thought about the irony of hosting a party featuring a game I sucked at. It was like hosting a pie party with burnt-up pie. Or a hat party while wearing a stained and faded baseball cap.

"What do you do all day, then?" another girl asked.

"Not much. I look around a lot, listen to sounds. Watch the sun rise and set." It sounded histrionic, but I was just summarizing.

That was the end of talking. No one had much to say on those topics. Before, I thought they were boring, and now I was boring. I wished I were at an animal party.

Toward the end of the night, my neighbor Mildred called. She was ninety-three and survived on a respirator. She'd lived her whole life in the desert working as a waitress at the local diner. Sometimes she'd call me if her oxygen cords were tangled around the leg of a table, or if she needed a hand moving the boxy air machine. But this time she called to warn me.

"Is your cat in?" she asked.

"I don't have a cat anymore, remember?" I answered sadly.

"Well, the bobcat's making its way up the street, and it's headed for your yard," she said. "That same one came around here about five years ago and got Hal's cat. Lock the door and you'll be all right."

I thanked her for calling and hung up. I'd always wanted to see a wildcat close up. We stopped playing Burgertime and killed the lights. This was enough action to impress my city friends, and we rolled another joint. Once we were settled and stoned, the cat wandered up casually onto the patio, and stared in my window. It had pointy fuzz on its ear tips and was three times as big as a house cat. Orangish-brown coat with slight stripes. Everyone had a peek, then went back to talking. Their chattering annoyed me.

I kept peering out until the bobcat and I finally made eye contact. I tried not to blink. The intensity of relating to a wildcat gave me mystical dreams for weeks. I dreamed about being half-human, half-animal—mixed genera. When I spoke, meows came out. Not even my parents understood me.

In one dream I lived with woodrats under a boulder. I sat there naked and shivering while I watched them nestle into their rough bed, huddling together in a furry, warm mass. They winked at me with their long black eyelashes looking glamorous in the breeze that was freezing me.

* * *

When your cat dies, sleeping feels so empty. It's that same emptiness you get when everything's predictable, planned. The running errands, empty. The not-enough-time-in-the-day, empty. You can't bury your hand in the cat's belly fur or pull its whiskers up to inspect the tiny fangs. Interaction with pets helps me sleep more soundly.

I got my first cat—the one who was run over—because she was free and cute. I lived alone, worked at a deli. In the evenings I'd make her cat-sized sandwiches with cheese, fish, kibble, cantaloupe, bologna, peas, and other favorites. We ate out of the same dish. She had a triple-row turquoise and pink rhinestone collar that accentuated her blue eyes. We were both horny, but neither of us wanted to give it up for just anyone.

When you're female and single, a female single cat is a surrogate sister. Two innocent creatures, not virgins, just sweet. I hated my job and was so broke I didn't even open bills—just tossed them, sealed envelopes, into the dumpster. I bought an ice cream cone for my cat and I to lick. Cats serve as pillows. They pull weeds with you out in the garden, eat roaches and other bugs you hate to squash, and perform countless other duties—not every duty (like fixing broken light fixtures or taking the trash out), but enough. I don't need to convince everyone of how great cats are.

Lacking a cat combined with living in utter silence in the desert where there are no night sounds made me an insomniac. Video games are a treatment for this. That's how Burgertime saved me.

Playing Burgertime gives you this false sense of staying busy, as if you are personally responsible for delivering meat to mankind. Staving off starvation of the masses is an overwhelming task that requires total dedication. Catching the stuff on the bun takes on religious significance, as if it's manna floating down from heaven. Don't fuck up and drop the lettuce crooked on the burger or it will drift off the cliff beside you. As you read this, you think, *Who cares about Burgertime?* But when you're awake all night because it's too quiet and there's no cat to wiggle your foot on, your deluded brain mistakes the Chef's duties for your own. You'll be making burgers all night sometime—just watch.

Now I live in Los Angeles again with my new cat, an orange tabby. Last month, a friend and I went to the desert to camp and watch shooting stars. Driving in night wilderness with the high beams on, we saw an animal scurry across the road. Since I thought we were going to hit it, I yelled, *Go kitty go!*, thinking it was a cat. But a domestic cat wouldn't be in the middle of the desert. My mind had automatically gone into cat mode.

When you go into cat mode, everything relates to your pet cat. When you walk past an aromatic shrub, you think, *My cat would love that smell.* You'll wake up from a dream with a physical craving to touch cat hair. Going into cat mode is usually fine and entertaining, nothing too psychological. But death and nighttime complicate cat mode.

I think of my cats when I see the moon, since throughout history cats have represented the moon in its various feminine forms. The goddess Diana transformed herself into a cat when Typhon forced the gods to adopt animal shapes in order to flee to Egypt. Diana traveled using moonlight to hide herself, thus associating the image of a sneaky cat crawling across the night with witchcraft. In the ancient Eastern world in which cats were worshipped, a coiled cat reminded people of the moon cycle and the divine darkness of nature.

When I dream about the bobcat, its eyes turn gold and its fur turns black, silhouetted by cold light. Is it the proverbial Black Cat—"the cat who symbolizes that which is uncreated, the vast deep unknown, the limitless, formless, and inexpressible"[1]? I think back to the bobcat and wonder if it was a witch shape-shifted to illustrate some mystery.

A bit of witch trivia—Isobel Gowdie, known as the queen of Scottish witches, was condemned to death in 1662 after revealing her spell that changed women into cats:

> I shall goe intill ane catt,
> With sorrow, and sych, and a blak shott;
> And I shall goe in the Divellis nam,
> Ay quhill I com hom againe.

* * *

Now I never feel lonely, although I do frequently feel bored. This reminds me of an old friend who was so bored he got hooked on swimming with alligators. He was in Louisiana, near waterways where he could see the beasts surfacing and plunging down, disappearing. Every time he saw one, he'd take a swig of whiskey and jump on in. This was his cure for boredom. Will I one day be tying slabs of smoked salmon onto myself, sitting in alleys downtown waiting for feral dogs to gnaw me?

If I feel lonely, I have my cat and I have my friends. If humans don't work, and one cat isn't enough (as is often the case), I can still throw animal parties with skunks, raccoons, hawks, and possums. I miss my black widow.

My tabby loves skunks. She's a mini-bobcat. I observe her in staring contests, and try to translate her hisses during late-night showdowns. Her eyes get slitted, turn iridescent gold, and her fur magically gets more auburn. The bristling displays her dark undercoat. I like to think of her slinking up tree trunks, pawing through grass, and catching baby snakes. But I also like it when she curls up like a cinnamon bun in my lap while I sit inside playing Burgertime.

[1] *The Cat in Magic*, M. Oldfield Howey.

BIENVENIDO EL DUENDE

Dear Elf,

I was nine when I saw my dad placing presents under the Christmas tree in the middle of the night. The next morning I recognized my mother's cursive on the gift tags labeled FROM: SANTA. I'd known it all along. That's all I could think as I rode my Powder Puff Big Wheel around on the living room carpet. That's pretty advanced thinking for a nine-year-old girl overwhelmed by piles of gifts, but I remember these thoughts. Still, sometimes I wonder, Could I really have been so savvy? Sometimes I imbue my younger self with an intelligence that couldn't possibly have fruited. I'm also assuming elves are literate. I've always pictured you smarter than us, even as children.

Anyway, after that real or imagined revelation, I

just told my parents what I wanted for Christmas and got it over with. Santa was over; my slim hope that fantasy beings dwelled on Earth had been crushed. I felt defeated. Before my revelation, I was an elf busied by beliefs in the supernatural; then all at once I morphed into an adult human. I grew hairy armpits and a small shrub below.

"Define the difference between REALITY and WISHFUL THINKING." This was one of the many lessons that taught me fun and reality are indirectly linked. Maturity is a series of depressing realizations that what you wish for will not necessarily come true. Christmas is meant to be a remedy. It's a distracting holiday—people temporarily forget their woes and allow themselves to be swept away by the Christmas Spirit. But why should we pretend to be happy?

Sincerely,

Human

Dear Human,

Thank you for assuming elves are literate. Most elves are born with the ancient language already within them. We can read and write in our cribs. It is not uncommon for elders to converse at length with their babies on such topics as philosophy and math.

On the topic of celebrating depressing concepts, I've never understood the Catholic habit of feast days to commemorate martyrs such as St. Nicholas.

I don't understand martyrdom. What is so honorable about dying in prison, starving oneself, being burned alive, or dying of lye poisoning, for example, as was the case with my own baptismal saint, Rose of Lima?

It's true, I'm a Catholic elf. There are a few of us up here who have church-going parents. I happen to think going to church is the dullest pastime in the world, especially when the option of slinging gifts over Santa's back entices me. Our church is very small; the spire is only thirty feet tall, and it's the tallest building in the village.

By the way, fantasy beings dwell on Earth in two forms: elves and gnomes. The gnome race is near extinction. The few remaining clans live in isolated pockets of pine forest—I can't reveal exact locations. Elves live in cold regions. But to be accurate, fantasy beings by definition do not exist. Are you hopeless because your fantasies cannot be realized?

Merry Christmas,

Elf

Elf,

Talking to a baby about the meaning of life must be satisfying. Thank you for the tips on elves versus gnomes. If you can't reveal village locations, can you send me a picture of yourself? Do you have a portrait you could spare? I imagine it would warrant a tiny picture frame. You must be a very cute man. Not to insult your manhood . . . I've only seen caricatures of

elves: adorable green creatures with elaborate outfits. I'm amazed you wrote back!
Human

Dear Human,

Why bother to write someone if you don't hope they'll write back? I don't expect humans to write me back, but I do *hope* they will. It's an innocent excitement. Enclosed is a picture of me on my 200th birthday. I have a few gray hairs that used to be green, but our greens are browner than the ones humans associate with elves. My hair used to be a ruddy green, more like the back of a bullfrog than that of the vibrant grass growing in meadows.

Do you still think "fun and reality are indirectly linked"? Maybe you should visit the toy factory here. We eat candy and sing songs all day. And why not try writing to me about something I can relate to—like toys, snow, reindeer, or presents?
Hopefully,
Elf

Dear Elf,

You are so distinguished looking! Let's start over. I am a middle-aged American woman, 140 lbs, 5'8". How tall are you? Are your striped tights red and white? Do you attend elf school, or do you work in the North Pole Post Office? Who do like better, Mrs. Claus or Santa?

To answer your question about reality, I'm saying that Christmas is a lie. Times that are supposed to be fun and aren't are more devastating than times that you know won't be fun, because hopes are crushed. Every holiday, especially Christmas, I think hope will sprinkle down on my head like snowflakes; just a few tiny flakes would suffice. I actually imagine hope as snow: crystalline, elusive, beautiful, unmistakable. People here hate snow because it's depressing, but I've always thought hope is stored in snowstorms.

Only recently have I begun to give up believing that good things will happen to me. All year long I work hard, but I'm underpaid. Bills stack up; I'll never have money to own a house or car. I'm ugly with long, straggly hair that's beginning to fall out. I keep it dyed black to look younger. Sometimes I fear I'm doomed to become as vicious as Mommie Dearest.

There's no wish list attached here. I have given it considerable thought and decided that to wish too many things at once can only invite disaster. I'm taking some advice of yours—hope your wishes will come true. I have already wished that elves were real, and my wish came true. So I'm putting a lot of faith in you, Elf, for three reasons: you wrote me back twice, sent me a photo, and you're Catholic, which seems significant. I'm working on Earth wishes this year, more concrete things, and if that goes well, I'll wish for universal things in the future.

Please write back!

Human

Dear Human,

Another elf told me that some humans think Santa is Satan in disguise, since their names share the same letters. Is this true? Santa would of course disagree. Are you a Satan worshipper, and is that why you've been sending me such bizarre letters? If you are, please stop writing me. If you hate your life, why not end it? Suicide is plausible in elf culture. If there is an elf in crisis, we take him to the Supreme Elf Counselor in order to determine whether or not he can be alleviated of his pains. Then an Elf Council votes on his right to end his own life. Catholic Elves dispute this, but suicide has traditionally been the most merciful way to end misery. Very few elves wish to kill themselves, however. Only the males are allowed to contemplate it.

To answer your question about which Claus I favor, I can't answer that because Santa pays my salary and provides my family with food and cheer. Mrs. Claus brings trays of brownies and Pfeffernüsse to us while we're toiling on the gift assembly line. Did you know each gift is not custom-crafted but rather mass-produced? I hope I haven't caused any disillusionment by revealing this secret.

You said you used to believe in fantasy creatures when you were a child, and now you are writing to an elf. How has your hope been crushed?
Merry Christmas,
Elf

Dear Elf,

I may be a descendant of the Vikings (I'm of
Scandinavian origin), but I am not a devil worshipper. Thor is my own personal master: the god of
thunder, the strongest supreme being alive. Thor is
the real Santa Claus. In legends, he is old and robust,
has a long white beard, and dresses in a red suit. His
chariot is powered by two white goats, Cracker and
Gnasher, who carry him to his palace in the North.
No wonder, then, that your Claus stuffs himself
down chimneys toward the hearth, the fire center.
Fire is Thor's element! How do you carry on knowing
the man to whom you've dedicated your life's work is
a fake? He probably glues on his beard and shoves a
pillow under his coat to make his belly bulge.

I wasn't writing you a suicide note—if I wanted to
die, I'd be dead already. I wouldn't be wasting my
time corresponding with elves. Here's why I wish
fantasies could become reality: because they're so
much more interesting. Manticores and mermaids
are more appealing than goldfish and rats. In daily
life, even if you see something you've never seen
before, it can't beat a minotaur shooting arrows into
a mushroom cloud. I wish an army of skeletons
would swordfight me like they did Jason in *Jason and
the Argonauts*. What would be the most surprising
thing that could happen to me today? A spider biting
me? Big deal.

Writing to you gives me great consolation, I must

say. I am not accusing you of being a fraud, I'm only telling you that you've got options. Have you ever visited Los Angeles? You are welcome here. I live in a predominantly Hispanic neighborhood, so bring a Spanish dictionary. In Spanish, you are El Duende. If you come, you are invited to my house and can stay indefinitely.

Do the Claus's have an heir to the throne, or is Santa supposedly immortal? How many old geezers posing as Santa live among you? I ask you these confidential details only because you volunteered information in your previous letter that shocked me and confirmed the reality of this correspondence. No false elf would have the mind or the brazenness to concoct a story about toy quality in Santa's workshop. I guess if Santa found out, you'd be fired. Your confidence leads me to believe you are high in the Order of Elves, and Santa favors you. Do you perhaps tend to the reindeer barn and otherwise govern animals? I have a set of reindeer antlers hung on the porch above the front door to greet visitors.

Truthfully yours,

Human

Dear Noble Viking,

Thank you for your invitation. I do frequently visit the reindeer barn because I'm a veterinarian and physician. I am Santa's personal doctor. (He gets several colds per season, and is gout-ridden.) Since I hold a degree in Ancient Chemistry, I brew my own medicines and curatives and am licensed to operate when necessary, using elf laser procedures far superior to your techniques. Santa is a hemophiliac; when he bleeds, his blood is a dark, thick red that fascinates me and makes me want to taste it. Do you drink blood, Viking? I imagine your chalice dedicated to that ceremony. What if an elf drank human blood? I have heard vampires drink blood and live at night. Pagan elves believe vampires are cursed elves doomed to eternal suffering.

No human has ever invited me into her home; only Santa receives that sort of hospitality. You and I are not as far apart geographically as I envisioned. I can hop the southbound sleigh easily. I'll stow away in the red velvet pockets that store Santa's maps, handkerchief, and whiskey.

I have no real family as I boasted before. All I am bringing is my medicine bag, spectacles, and a few wool sweaters. I can bring you elf wine as an offering. I am comfortably fed with a mouse steak, halved green peas or grains of rice, and other small, healthy foods. I will be useful for tasks like locating lost earrings in the carpet or removing bee stingers. I can do anything gnomes do but with more accuracy. Elves are more intelligent than gnomes.

See you soon,

Elf

CHRYSALIS

Four girlfriends and I stayed up watching *Nightmare on Elm Street* until the first pink streaks in the sky appeared. Then we dressed in sweats and headed out to TP the church down the street. I had fun throwing rolls of Charmin over the trees, but the chapel was much too large to huck toilet paper over. I'd planned to do the giant cross; I'd envisioned it littered with white, soggy streamers when churchgoers arrived Sunday morning, and the image was beautiful to me. It made a festive statement, as if church wasn't just a deadly boring place that sucked ass and hated children. Since we couldn't throw the TP high enough to lace the cross, we took pictures of ourselves making out on the church lawn, thereby defacing the sacred grounds with homosexuality.

To prepare for the attack, we snuck bottles of

Malibu and Bailey's from the liquor cabinet, stole a jar of whole cloves off the spice rack and smoked them in rolled-up post-it notes, then applied slut makeup to wear on the journey. I owe it all to Freddy Kruger.

Six of us were lying around on the floor, watching a girl walk down the upstairs hall in her dead friend's house, opening each door slowly to check for clues. I was half watching the movie and half hating my pre-algebra teacher. She had poodle hair and a huge ass that disfigured her polyester pants.

"You know," I said, "having a teacher that isn't butt ugly would really improve math class. Fat teachers should be illegal."

Everyone ignored me. "Why do they always do exactly what I *wouldn't* do if Freddy was in the house?" my friend asked.

"I know, it's not even scary. She's so stupid you want her to die," another girl said.

"Um, does that mean you guys like math?" I asked. "You like looking at Mrs. Ferret's big-ass ass?"

"Stop talking about asses," someone mumbled.

Blood splattered on the camera lens.

By then, we had seen Freddy kill one too many people. The moon was bright, and it lit the shrubbery while we gazed out windows to devise a plan.

"We could go skinny-dipping," one girl said as she looked out at the dark swimming pool.

"Oh yeah, let's stare at each other naked," someone snapped back.

"You are so lesbian," I said.

"Well then, let's dress up like lesbians and sneak into the church," someone said. No one disagreed, so we did.

The first time a slumber party actually turned bad was when this skinhead, a friend's older sister's boyfriend, locked me in the bathroom and told me to strip. He was teaching me how to chop lines. He pressed me up against the mirrored wallpaper and I felt like there was someone behind me, sandwiching me in, because his reflection showed up in my peripheral vision. His breath smelled like he'd been drinking B.O.

"Come on, let me feel them," he said, forcing his hands up my shirt.

"It's 3 in the morning, and your girlfriend is out there sleeping. Don't you think this is a little weird?" I asked.

"She doesn't care."

"I'm too young for you," I offered. I was thirteen, he was twenty.

I thought of my sleeping bag, covered with Snoopies and Belles, Snoopy's twin dog girlfriend, and how it should have had me inside it. It should have been keeping me warm that very minute. Instead, a guy was pushing me against a towel rack.

"Ow! You're hurting me. Let me go," I said through my teeth.

"Be quiet," he said. I could feel his hard-on on my hipbone.

"Let go or I'll scream," I said finally.

I wandered back down the hall and crawled into my sack, happy to be surrounded by my sleeping girlfriends. Picturing Snoopy and his gentle female companion, I petted my sleeping bag's flannel lining in the dark.

Another time, two years later, I went to a super lame slumber party where the mom tried too hard by making bowls of "brains" out of cold, cooked spaghetti, and "eyeballs" out of frozen grapes. Theme parties were out of style. To plan anything out, especially if it was supposed to be scary, was the most uncool thing ever. We watched *Halloween* and took turns in the kitchen making English muffin pizzas. During my solo muffin shift, I was spooning on tomato sauce while imagining it was bloody guts, and I got the idea to set one out on the porch as a snack that would attract killers. The party needed a boost.

I made an extra muffin, put it out on a paper towel behind the potted petunias on my friend's porch, and went back inside to watch the movie. Michael Myers wandered stiffly through backyards on the screen. Once in a while I looked out the window to see if a man in a mechanic's suit was feasting on the pizza.

"What are you looking for?" my friend asked.

"I'm just seeing if anyone's out there," I replied.

"You're afraid!" They all laughed.

"I'm just bored. Let's go out or something. I've seen this movie a million times."

We got dressed and drove the parents' car up to the Haunted Forest, an abandoned estate at the top of a street that dead-ended at the beginning of mountainous foothills. Wrought-iron gates guarded the world where an eccentric millionaire had lived during Victorian times. There were relics, like the house's crumbled foundation and random bricks scattered in the dirt, and it was a great party spot.

The moon was out, not full but bright enough to help us reach a hill above the old house. We had some wine coolers and a joint to smoke. Sitting around on the rocks, checking out the view, we were pretty chill until two dark human shapes appeared on the trail we'd just taken. Then two guys stood in front of us, blocking our way down.

They made conversation with us—where we were from, what school we went to, what we liked to drink. They wouldn't really leave us alone. They were our parents' age—bearded, gruff like bikers. By the time they started getting creepy, only one girl was still talking to them, probably because she was afraid to shut up.

"Do you girls have underwear on?" one guy asked. We all giggled nervously, and said yeah, duh, of course.

The other guy was silent now, but he had the most evil energy. His silhouette in the moonlight was darker than his buddy's. His shadow was longer on the ground, too.

The evil guy said, in a lowered voice, "If you show 'em to us, we'll let you girls get back to your party."

I offered to show him my underwear, but nothing else. *You can't even touch it*, I said. I wanted them to go away, and this was the quickest way. We made a deal, and I presented from under my long skirt a pair of dark pink satin underwear that had small ruffled fringes around the seams. Small white polkadots, too, that glowed in the dark. I'd just got them at the mall a few weeks before. They'd looked so cute in the store, but now the dots took on this sickly appearance, as if the panties had measles.

He took the underwear from me and rubbed the back of his hand on them. We all sat quietly, waiting to see what he'd do next. He spat in them, a big loogie, not just spittle, then rubbed it around and handed them back.

"Put 'em on," he said firmly.

I pulled them halfway on, thinking he'd never know, but he told me to lift up my skirt to make sure they were pulled all the way up. He brushed his paw against my crotch to make sure the spit was touching it. I was so pissed, but totally quiet. After all, I could take a shower when we got back.

The next day on the phone, in hushed tones behind locked bedroom doors, we talked about how twisted those guys were, how disgusting and perverted and pathetic men could be, and how desperate they must have been. There was no real issue of whether or not I was all right, because he hadn't hurt me. I just kept thinking about how slimy the spit was, and I tried not to picture it—brown and dark yellow, like men's loogies are when they smoke. I pictured my under-wear out in the road where I'd tossed them from the car window. I saw them being driven over by car after car. I thought, if I ever saw that underwear on the rack at a department store I'd rush to the bath-room. Worst of all, I pictured the guy home alone afterwards, thinking of my crotch and getting busy in his loser armchair.

It's not that I was afraid to watch horror movies after that, but we just got out of the habit because we were always sneaking out to get drunk instead of staying home in our pajamas like a bunch of pussies. Sleeping bags are like cocoons—teenage girls are the pupae. We lay around in warm sacks awaiting meta-morphosis so we could buy bras with bigger cup sizes.

As an older teenager, I thought back to the slum-ber party days and wished we'd done more things at home that we'd seen in the movies, like have pillow fights in our lingerie. But we didn't even have lin-gerie. Did polka-dotted pink panties count? I didn't think so. I didn't understand what steps I'd missed. We went straight from watching gory movies to get-ting bored with gory movies to getting drunk or high because we were bored. But now that I wanted the innocence back, I couldn't get it. Pillow fights were fake and stupid. Flipping through yearbooks was fine, but it wasn't a Friday night activity. Mostly, I just wanted to hang with my girlfriends, smoke weed, and not be harassed.

Now when I watch *Slumber Party Massacre* or *The Last Slumber Party*, and I see girls chewing gum with their tits bobbing up and down beneath their cropped T-shirts while wearing their whitest, cleanest panties, I trip out on how they seem so carefree and cheerful while getting their lives interrupted by men who can't control themselves. I think of a reverse chrysalis—like they're kids who come out of a paradisiacal state only to enter their own personal hell. I didn't like being ensnared, but now I appreciate watching it happen on screen—I feel pleasantly satisfied knowing the girls' fates ahead of time, almost as if I'm the killer. I know that he wants the same thing I do, to see girls at their cutest.

TILES

Did you ever see that picture of the mouse with a human ear stitched onto its back? The sight of bloodied tiles can be abhorrent like that. There's nothing like something beyond disgusting, something that scars you mentally.

I.

When I was five, my mom and I kneaded two loaves of bread. It was my job to find a place on the hall floor where the dough could rise in peace. It had to be a spot where my basset hound wouldn't find the oiled pans full of salty dough and eat them. It had to be away from foot traffic because too much noise could stunt the fluffy, white, sticky bundles I was aiming for. My mom told me to hide them overnight and check on them periodically. I didn't sleep that night because every twenty minutes I was jumping out of bed to make sure they were safe.

I was sitting beside my loaves, trying to watch them rise, when I heard a loud thump in the bathroom and ran in. My dad was lying on the floor, head propped up against the bathtub. There was blood on the sink and smeared in the basin. Trickles of blood ran down my dad's face and neck. His black hair looked matted like a rabid dog's. There were blood squiggles on the floor tiles, too. It wasn't pink like in cartoons, it was brown. Brick-red and streaky.

Years later, my mom told me Dad had come home drunk from a bar and slipped on the bathroom's slick floor. After that, we got lots of bathmats and those rough vinyl flowers called flower daisies that stick on your shower floor. Nothing was ever slippery again.

II.

My brother's old house was a partially converted laundromat. He and about ten other college-aged guys lived in the warehouse area behind a fully operational laundromat. They paid rent by working shifts, watching customers and collecting quarters, making sure dryers were lint-free and running hot.

Their kitchen was never used. Mice lived in the stove. Beer cans, cigarette butts, and bottles littered the countertops, and the pantry was stocked with jugs of cheap wine. It smelled like hobos lived there. When I asked my brother why the kitchen reeked so bad, he told me it was because they used the sink as a urinal.

The shower worked, but was mildewy. Between the tiles, the caulking was black. Maybe the tiles had been white, but they were moldy now.

One of his friends was taking a shower, scrubbing with a bar of soap and making lots of suds. He aimed his piss stream down into the drain, and the combination of hot, bitter liquid and massive soap residue caused a mutant salamander to emerge. It had been living in the drain, shower after shower, month after month. Soap scum and other human skin chunks had built up on its back, and it had bumps that looked irregular like warts, or like someone had sewn on genetically fucked-up appendages.

The boy rinsed off in a panic as he watched the amphibian creeping toward his feet. It was ruddy and black-green, like a four-inch-long crocodile. It might have been poisonous. He was afraid to touch it, but it was too quick for him. It crawled onto his foot. Reflexively he shook it off and squished it, as if it were a cockroach. But after the stomp, he had to hit it again with the shampoo bottle to fully kill it. Its flesh, blood, intestines, and textured skin mixed with his dirty suds, creating a crimson wash that forever stained the shower floor. No one got anywhere near those tiles again.

III.

My friend Rick was in medical school. He'd returned home from his anatomy class, preoccupied with upcoming assignments revolving around dissecting his first human cadaver. He was studying to be a doctor, so this was something he looked forward to. Still, you can imagine it might induce a few nightmares, or at least some apprehensive thoughts. He decided to run a bath. It was late autumn and the air in his apartment was chilly. To alleviate stress, he poured three capfuls of Avon's Skin So Soft bath oil under the spigot, which is surprising since it's not a very masculine product.

He took his bath like a Calgon model: soaked himself and closed his eyes, leaned back, submerged his head momentarily, rubbed his hairy chest with bath gel. His towel was laid out on the floor next to him, ready to grab. As he stood up and was bending over to get his towel, one foot flew out from under him. (Mineral oil, if you've never used it, leaves a film on your bathtub that can only be removed with Ajax cleanser.) He lurched forward, grabbed for the faucet but missed and fell, and was stabbed by the hot water knob. His rib cage caught on the knob, and not only did the handle pierce the skin, it was torn out again as he fell down, breaking his bottom left rib.

The water hadn't drained yet. Blood smeared down the faucet and tinted the water pink. The worst part, he told me, was that the oily patches on the surface of the water absorbed more blood and floated around him like red lilypads. He said he felt like he was suspended in his own blood stream, surrounded by erythrocytes. A doctor's perspective, certainly.

IV.

Two close friends of mine were filming a sequence involving a stalker coming down a flight of stairs clutching a gigantic knife. He was headed for a bright-tiled kitchen where a young girl cringed in fear. The filmmaker focused the camera on the maniac walking slowly down carpeted stairs, and he continued filming as the murderer lost his footing and fell on his knife, which penetrated his thigh so deeply it poked out the backside. The wounded murderer limped into the kitchen, leaving a trail of bloody footprints on the tiled floor. He had on work boots with heavy treading, which left arrow-like patterns pointing to him. At that point, all filming ceased. The director rushed into the kitchen where his friend was slumped awkwardly against the stove, and together they pulled the knife from his leg.

The knife severed a main artery, so blood squirted out at intervals relative to his body's pulse. He almost bled to death. He couldn't walk for weeks. A surgeon had to slice in there and tie the artery off. The knife was saved as a grim souvenir and added to the huge collection of knives they had around the house. One of them was an unsuccessful salesman for CUTCO at the time. He had to buy all the knives he didn't sell. It was a door-to-door gig, but he couldn't stand to knock on doors and nag people. He actually lost money because he was forced to purchase knives. So his impetus for making thrillers stemmed from two facts: he had lots of knives, and he hated his job.

* * *

Tiles serve to accentuate the color of blood, as well as give blood a surface to expand on, whether it forms beaded droplets, thick round drip lines, or thin smears. I've seen opaque smears, mostly in movies, because usually if a bleeding person is thrown against tile, their weight takes the majority of the gore down with them as they slink into a crippled pile. I've cut my leg shaving before, and if I touch the sliced area to the tiled wall, it merely leaves a rust-colored spot, which I immediately have to rinse off to avoid nausea. If you make a horror movie, please use tiles. They're a cliché now, especially after Alfred Hitchcock's *Psycho*, but one needn't use a foot-long blade in shadow to instill fear in the viewer. Make a tiled house interior, wall-to-wall, and see what transpires. Apply mineral oil to every ceiling, wall, doorjamb, appliance, and piece of furniture. Insist all the actors perform nude. And let me know when I can see it.

THE WOOKIEE SAW MY NIPPLES
A WEEK IN THE LIFE OF PRINCESS LEIA

Monday

The boy we elected Han Solo in the sandbox last Tuesday is the most popular boy at school. I like him but not that much. I wanted Richard to win, but I was out-voted by six other girls. Anyways, I was on the bars and looked down and noticed my nipples were hanging out of my dress, so I got embarrassed and went inside. I think Han Solo saw them because he poked me with his light saber three times today at recess even though I was playing with Max. Max has red hair and eats his boogers, which is gross. But I like Max because he doesn't go around thinking he's so great. He's shy and most of the sounds he makes are truck noises as he's pushing his yellow dump trucks around. Han Solo talks all the time. He even talked in class today after Miss Kelly told him to be quiet. She was asking Lily how many red triangles she could find on the page in the book we were reading. Han said there were no red triangles and everyone started laughing. I raised my hand and said six, so Miss Kelly gave me two extra stars on the class chart. If I get fifteen more I can have a free pass to recess five minutes before everybody else. That's how I get dibbs on the best swing or on the handball that isn't lumpy.

Tuesday

Han Solo is so mean! I hate his guts. This morning I wrote a note to my friend Alissa and I folded it up and put like ten stickers on it so no one would read it as they passed it along. The note was about Han. I asked if she thought he was cute or not. I think he's all right, but if I could choose Han Solo I would still pick Richard because he has light-blue eyes that are like space eyes. He looks like he would be from space and know lots of aliens, like in that bar in *Star Wars* when the aliens are playing music and there's that blue one playing the horn that looks like an elephant. Remember when Han is in the bar and Chewie talks to him and Han knows exactly what Chewie's saying? The average person wouldn't know because Chewie's language is from space. But it seems like Richard would know.

Anyways, I asked Han to pass the note to Alissa so Miss Kelly wouldn't see. Most people will hide a note in their lap, and if Miss Kelly asks to see it they just drop it between their legs onto the floor. That's a trick Richard learned from a fifth grader. He showed it to us, and I thought Han knew it but he didn't. Miss Kelly took the note from Han and now I have minus five stars on my chart. Even Max is beating me. Max has the fewest stars because Miss Kelly keeps telling him not to pick his nose, but he does anyway. He should stop because almost nobody likes him.

So now Han knows I like Richard better and he probably hates my guts too!

Wednesday

Yesterday I was elected Princess Leia. Everybody stood around in the playhouse and decided with me standing right there. It was embarrassing. Han Solo picked me. It makes sense because he has to pick someone he likes or else they won't make a good couple. Alissa told me Han picked me because I have long dark hair like Leia's and am kind of cute! I'm not supposed to know. So I can't act like I like Han because then he'll know I know. At least now he doesn't hate me, and I guess I don't hate him as much because he started being really nice. Here's what it was like in the playhouse today:

"Leia, come to the top level with me. We have to save Chewie, he's trapped by Imperial Storm Troopers," Han said.

"Wait," I said, "let me change into my white robe."

"There's no time!" Han yelled as he climbed the ladder. "Chewie's dying!"

Then he came over and put his arm around my waist and pulled me away from the closet. He gave me a kiss on the cheek and said, "Leia, take my hand!" Then he held my hand and helped me get up the ladder that goes to the roof. It's small up there and there's only room for two people. Usually whoever play Han and Leia get to go up there, sometimes Luke or Chewie, so I'd never seen the view. Han Solo sat next to me and said to look at the galaxy because one day it was going to get exploded by Darth. It was so sad and romantic. Then he kissed me on the lips.

Thursday

Han Solo is my boyfriend now! It all makes sense because I am Leia, so that's how it really should be anyway. He hasn't asked to see my nipples again but we've kissed four times so if he asks, I might show him. I asked Alissa if I should or not.

"If Han wants to look at my nipples, do you think I should let him?"

"You're Leia. You have to," she said. "Otherwise you might get voted out."

"But don't you think Miss Kelly would find out because Han would tell everybody?" I asked.

"Maybe, but then Richard will know everything and he might like you more," she said.

"Why?" I asked.

"Because if the teacher knows and you get in trouble, Richard will think you're cool," she explained. "He likes girls who get in trouble."

That made me like Richard more because he isn't as nerdy as Han. Han is nice, but he sometimes seems sort of like a nerd. He's a teacher's pet. Like every day he beats the erasers outside to clean the chalk off for Miss Kelly. He has the most stars.

So I decided if Han asks, I will show him what he wants because he is technically my boyfriend. I'm thinking about breaking up, though. Richard is cooler and he's not such a goody goody.

Friday

This morning when I was lined up against the classroom wall waiting for the bell to ring, Han Solo came over and started talking about how his wookiee wanted to meet me on the upper level at recess as soon as the bell rang. So when we got out for nutrition break I ran over there, climbed the ladder, and untucked my shirt so it could be lifted up easily. My mom makes me tuck it in but I always untuck it, so it's not just that I was doing it for Han. Anyways, I don't even know for sure if he saw my nipples that first time. It just seemed like it. He kept poking me in this weird, mean way. And my mom told me that sometimes boys will act mean even when they really like me. She said they're too afraid to say it. But then the next day Han kissed me, so I don't know what to think. Maybe he saw my nipples when we were climbing the ladder that first time. He was looking up and holding my hand, so he could've peeked if he tried.

I was on the upper level waiting. Then up came

Han, but he brought Chewie with him! I thought we were going to be alone. Chewie was handcuffed. Han told me he'd just rescued him from the Death Star and that they'd barely survived. Chewie roared because it's against the rules to speak. I noticed Chewie had dirty fingers and wondered why. But I was too nervous to ask.

"Leia, please locate the key to unlock these cuffs," Han said. I like him better when he's bossy. I started looking on the floor and picked up an imaginary key.

"Unlock my wookiee," he said as Chewie roared again. I set him free.

"Han, is Chewie going to stay here?" I asked. "Or do you think we should transfer him to Sector 7-B, where he can take a bath and eat?"

"Chewie has permission to stay," Han said. And Chewie put his hand on my hair, brushing it as if he had a big hairy paw. I didn't like this at all and pulled away.

Han asked his wookiee to turn around while he asked Leia something. Then Han whispered to me that if I could pull up my shirt and show his wookiee it might make Chewie feel better. Chewie was sick because Darth had tortured him with needles and hot metal. I knew it! I knew he had seen my nipples that time! I couldn't wait to tell Alissa.

"I am at your command," I said. "But the wookiee must face away." Then I gave him a kiss. He granted my wish and told Chewie to stay turned around with his eyes closed.

I lifted my shirt and Han looked for a second then

reached out to feel them. He didn't say anything, but he felt them with his fingers, a rub then a pinch. It hurt when he pinched but I didn't say *Ouch!* I didn't want him to think I couldn't handle it. I remembered that part where Leia makes a movie of herself and plays it through R2-D2 saying, *Help me, Obi Wan Kenobi, you're my only hope.* She was so brave. Then, in the trash compactor scene, her braids fell out but she didn't even care. Her hair was all messed up but she found a pole anyway and jammed up the walls that were about to mash everybody. I wondered, *What would Leia do?* I decided she would let Han squeeze her nipples as much as he wanted to. So he pinched mine pretty hard but it was kind of cool.

Then Chewie turned around and stared at me. I pulled my shirt down really fast. I was not Leia for a minute. I wanted to push him off the upper level into the sand. But I just stood strong and waited until Chewie climbed down the ladder, smiling the whole way like he was about to laugh. Han was about to laugh too, so I dumped him.

SOFT DEAD THINGS

I crave something to pet. I mean something besides my dog or cat. I need something even softer. My cat has a velvety coat, but it's not wispy and fine like a rabbit or rodent. Rubbing my nose in her soft, white belly fur makes me sneeze. Sometimes when I wake up, I'll kiss my dog's snout, but it unnerves me to think of the trash and hairy testicles it's been rooting around in. Still, he gets a morning smell I like, and sometimes I get off on his musky, bushy mane.

Right before I got my learner's permit, I took some allowance and bought a sheepskin steering wheel cover, anticipating the day when I could cruise the mountain highways in my own car, gripping the puffy wheel. It was expensive but high quality, not to mention so squishy that I figured if I ever went camping and forgot my pillow, it would come in handy.

In high school, I gave my friends rides in the sheepskin mobile, until one too many of them compared me to Ed Gein. After that, I began to view my flocculent treasure as a symbol of blatant disrespect for mammalian life. I was honestly worried someone would report me to PETA.

I stored my steering wheel cover with the car jack and canvas tool bag, only pulling it out when I was driving in neighborhoods where no one could recognize me. I dreamt of road trips to Montana, a place where I imagined every truck had something wrapped around its cold wheel. "Where's yer steering wheel cover, girl?" some grizzly farmer would ask me. "It's freezing ass, you're gonna lose some fingers grabbing that bare wheel." I'd reach down and pull out my sheepskin, proudly stretch it around the wheel, then grip. "That's more like it," the burly guy would say, satisfied.

Eventually the sheepskin pilled with little balls of wool. In the spots where I held it, the fur rubbed completely off and the skin grew torn and holey. Still, I used it until the thing was threadbare.

Back when I was in kindergarten, I used to have a lot of tea parties. Once when I opened my teapot to inhale the imaginary steaming hot peppermint tea, I got a whiff of my hamster with her pissy nest-shavings stink. I decided she needed a bath. How cute she would look popping out of the teapot like a

Victorian children's book illustration—the china pot, the round brown hamster ears, its whiskers against a floral-print wallpaper (the decals on the kettle were roses). In my Beatrix Potter books there were no hamsters, but there were lots of mice, and they were always getting dirty then tidying up to stay out of trouble. I hallucinated Hunca Munca and Mrs. Tittlemouse getting snippy with my pet because she was so disheveled.

So in the upstairs bathroom I ran the tap water until it reached maximum hotness and filled my kettle. Then I submerged the hamster. She pressed her paws against the oblong rim and scratched at me with her sticky claws, so I took tissues and wrapped my fingers in them. Once I got her inside, she started moving in slow motion and panting. After a final squeaky noise, she died, then slunk down into the teapot, limp and slick.

I pet her dead wet body for a long time. My hamster's fur was wet-soft instead of dry-soft, which is sort of like the difference between rubber and velcro. Although I knew I'd done something mischievous, my fascination overcame any feeling of regret. Part of my pleasure came from the fact that I could pet her for so long—finally she was docile.

Before I buried the teapot with her inside behind a tall fence overgrown with clematis in the backyard, I touched her one last time. The moment when I felt her cold tough skin, like leftover chicken nuggets, has stayed with me up to the present. Her fur felt nice, but I preferred her alive.

* * *

Fur still makes me sad but excited, or it did until last week when I visited a fur shop in Beverly Hills to check out the coats. This shop carries both exotic and classic coats like mink and fox. Whenever I'm there, I remember my grandma's Silver Fox jacket that used to hang in her closet. I used to wonder why it almost never left the garment bag. Why didn't she wear it all the time? I wanted a fur coat, but not one like hers. It had all these fox tails dangling from the waist. She looked like Davy Crockett when she wore it—like a pioneer trying to be dressy.

To enter Samantha Furs in Beverly Hills, you have to get buzzed in. I always put on lipstick before ringing the bell, so they'll think I'm serious.

On my most recent trip, a lady greeted me with long fingernails painted a gruesome coffee brown—I mean, the caramel of diner brew, not a rich chocolate espresso hue.

"Can I help you?" she asked, following me around as I eyed the garments.

"Just looking," I said. "Do you have any beavers?"

"We just got some beavers in," she said happily. Her high heels clicked across the tile floor to an especially dark brown, floor length coat that was wired to the rack.

I looked at the price tag, $5,000. It probably took fifty beavers to piece that thing together. A hundred dollars per beaver. *Beavers are worth so much more than that*, I thought.

"It's gorgeous," I said. "Can I try it on?"

Later, as I left the shop, a coiffed lady walked by flaunting a white rabbit stole while carrying her Pomeranian in her arms. They were an advertisement: *Dead fur and live fur combine into my ultimate fur experience; don't you wish you could afford the dead?* And I thought, *Why is dead animal fur more expensive than live animal fur? My dog was free! Fuck everyone in Beverly Hills, I'm going home to pet my dog for the next four hours.*

Every time I leave the fur store with that familiar feeling of humiliation, I tell myself I'll never go back.

I am officially still turned on by fur. I'm also in awe of living animals and wish to celebrate their lives to the fullest. Soft dead things attract and repel me—but I've only succumbed that once. Until I can live someplace wild where there are several velveteen animal species to experience, I'm cutting myself off. Lately I've learned to squeeze the fleshy cheeks of my pets the way I squeezed my old steering wheel cover. I shake them back and forth as I tell them how much I love them and how cute they looked when they were newborns. I dig up their baby pictures from some dusty box in the basement and bring the photos upstairs to wave in their blissful faces. My cat licks the photos (for the taste of the salty emulsion), and my dog just hangs his tongue out and slobbers on them. My pets were softer when they were young, but I still love them. Most people think Lenny (in *Of Mice and Men*) crushed his mouse accidentally because he was too strong and clumsy, but I believe he crushed it on purpose because he couldn't stand how cute it was and he went crazy.

To be truthful, I can't wait until my pooch is a foxy red panda-jacket. Sometimes I contemplate where in the house I will place his tanned skin—in the hallway, or maybe in the most classic spot, before the fireplace? I imagine lying on my side, nude, drinking champagne and having sex to Barry White on the earthly remnants of his being. I picture a remote mountain cabin, the savory smoke from the birchwood log that just got chucked into the fire, and the four-pointed Chow Chow hide pinned like butterfly wings to the top of the A-frame's two-story tall wall across from the bunk beds. My husband hangs his raccoon-tail hat on the pegs while he takes his muddy boots off on the porch. I am wearing leather moccasins to keep my feet warm. My kitty sniffs under the stove for bacon drippings. And in this future of using my deceased animal friends as decorations and clothing, I feel closer to the animals, more a part of the kingdom than ever before. This skin trend can extend far beyond soft things, into smooth suedes, into cool hard leathers, then into other product realms such as antler chandeliers and carved-bone letter openers. But every creature will have died a natural death. The rich Pomeranian lady from Beverly Hills had it totally wrong.

A GIANT LOVES YOU
FEATURING MARC BOLAN

A pair of salamanders circle a mushroom then lick it. Funny, since salamanders only eat nymphs, worms, grubs, and flies. I wasn't expecting to see them at all on this frigid canyon hike. But there they are—brown, orange, and bumpy—nibbling at the soft brown gills lining the cap's underside.

When I crouch, I notice they're shivering. A frosty spray off the puddle to the left has built fuzzy ice beards on their chins. Frozen twigs and clovers look like miniature ice sculptures.

One salamander whips his tail up at the mushroom and snaps off a bite. It falls onto the ground where he can eat it gracefully. Still, he twitches and tries to claw the cold off himself, as if he's hallucinating from advanced frostbite.

His companion is wounded, possibly from a recent owl attack. Maybe they ruffled the grass while crossing a meadow. An owl swooped down, extended its talon, but missed and slashed his head from ear to ear.

I scoop up one of the critters to pet its belly. They're slow when cold, like tarantulas and snakes. Normally I like catching salamanders with my boyfriend Matt. He can make them magically appear. He's a salamander magnet. "You found it," he always says. But I know they smell his ankles and calves then paddle out of their wet caves toward his woody scent. He smells like forest. My own smell is no fun. It can't compete with the mixture he exudes: pine and dirt, with a little something rotten mixed in.

One rock star who thought a lot about salamanders was the late Marc Bolan. He was the most fantastic singer. Back when he was Tyrannosaurus Rex, Marc Bolan wrote a song called "Salamanda Palaganda" about Aztec ancestors visiting him while he rested by a river. The chorus goes:

Salamanda palaganda, oh palomino blue
Salamanda palaganda, June's buffalo too

Apparently salamanders in England are blue. Marc Bolan spent a lot of time singing and dreaming beside streams, so I deem him a reliable source of British river life information. You can tell by his songs that he was attentive to animals and universal truths. That's part of what makes him so lovable.

Matt looks a lot like Bolan, but he's more handsome. He also likes lying beside streams and visiting visionary relatives. His Cherokee great-great-grandmother once came to him in the form of a tree. Her wrinkles were the tree's bark. She sorted some things out for him then took off. *How cool to be related to trees*, he told me.

The salamanders in Southern California are brown-reddish-orange, the color of an overripe Bosc pear. Except for their bright-orange underbellies, they camouflage well in oak leaf compost and sycamore twigs. However, the first mature salamander I ever met was yellow, and his head was heart-shaped like a living Valentine.

I don't know much about anything, except being lonely. When I'm alone, like now, I realize how much Matt and I have discussed the fact that being alone isn't a bad thing. He says it's good because you can experience supernatural things and more easily communicate with animals and plants. I'm sure he's right. Once I saw a leaf on the end of a branch start glowing and make itself into an arrow. When I went the way it pointed, I found a nest of blue jays. Their antics entertained me all afternoon.

The salamanders who love my boyfriend's smell are California Newts, *Taricha torosa*. They're amphibians who lay eggs just below the surface of a stream. California Newts can afford to spend time out on the shady forest floor. I used to wonder why they go to the hassle of giving birth amid torrential currents. Then I found out their eggs need cold water to gestate.

Every time I question why animals act differently than we do, I feel so stupid and anthropocentric. Maybe the water is a lubricant. Picture it—eggs covered in a silvery mucous just sliding out your birth canal. The river would soothe your feverish, leathery skin. It would fill in the holes and distended tubes, dampen your itchy back bumps—not to mention quench your thirst. Still, in the next chaotic moment, when newborns swarmed around you, wouldn't you be worried they'd be whisked away downstream? I mean, how would you secure your babies? After doing some research, I found out this tricky situation isn't as tricky as you'd think, thanks to these special sticky egg sacs that bond everyone to rocks like the caulking in shower-tile cracks.

Salamanders have it all figured out.

Last week before he left town, Matt scored Marc Bolan's first two records. One has a great, bongo-frenzy version of "Salamanda Palaganda."

"Bolan's such a hippie," he said.

"Yeah, isn't that song being played backwards?" I asked.

We talked about how glad we were when the band changed its name from Tyrannosaurus Rex to T.Rex, and Bolan laid off the bongos. When T.Rex added an electric guitar for the album *Beard of Stars*, the music got more intense. Bolan's curly hair is so beautiful on that cover, and his powdered face makes him look rococo. Handsome overkill. Bolan must have known bliss.

Medieval bestiaries claimed that salamanders had the ability to withstand and even extinguish flames. Roman naturalist Pliny propagated this legend by writing, "Salamanders are so cold that they put fire out by the touch, as ice does."[1] Benvenuto Cellini was a Renaissance artist and colleague of Michelangelo. He once saw a lizard "sporting about in the midst of the hottest flames."[2] He was sitting near a campfire in his family cellar (?!) at the time. What a sexy lizard to perform fire-dancing! On the other hand, how lonely was Cellini to see animals flickering in his bonfire?

The Vatican used to store the sudarium (that famous face-cloth from the tomb of Jesus Christ) in a fireproof material known as "salamander wool."[3] This was later proven to be asbestos. Many ornamental granite and limestone salamanders grace cathedrals throughout Europe. Matt loves gargoyles. I wonder if he'd love stone salamanders.

Some people think salamanders are algae-ridden bottom slitherers. No way. Look at their round snouts! I would kiss them, but I'm afraid I'd get them sick. I get horny when I see one swimming into a crevice after crawling through leaves at the bottom of a pool. How pretty is that? Their curvy tails are spermlike, and their skin is so soft (out of water) that, I hate to say it, they feel like penises.

* * *

In *The Philosophical Transactions of the Royal Society of 1716*, it was recorded that,

> *A salamander on being thrown into the fire . . . swelled and vomited*
> *a store of thick slimey matter, which did put out the neighboring coals*
> *. . . thereby saving himself from the force of the fire for two hours . . .*
> *and afterward lived for nine months.*

If placed in danger, salamanders can secrete juices stored in their backs. I've seen them sweat while sitting in my hand, although it could have been residual water beads. Chamouni, a man known as the "Russian Salamander," thought he could exude magic sweat, but he died in 1828 while being roasted in an oven beside a leg of lamb.[4]

On a hike about a year ago, Matt picked up a salamander and tried to hypnotize it by rubbing the underside of its neck. I wished I were the salamander, small enough to sit in his palm. The salamander struggled, but I would've fallen asleep. There's something about wanting to be small for your heartthrob. I strive to feel cute and tiny, like a surprise present. I feel jealous of creatures less than ten inches long. It's not that I don't want to have presence. It's not about disappearing. If you're small and a giant loves you, you're safe. You're the mouse in the matchbox bed.

[1] *Natural History*, Pliny, Book X and LXXXVI.
[2] *Magic Zoo*, Peter Costello, p.130.
[3] *Magic Zoo*, p.131.
[4] *The Bestiary of Christ*, Louis Charbonneau-Lassay.

FUNGUS MENTAL TELEPATHY

I've seen the Flaming Lips perform lots of times, but only once did the drummer, Steven, send me psychic messages to marry him. I felt lust recumbent in the dark, smoky air. His brainwaves were overpowering—during "It's Halloween on the Barbary Coast," they visually matched the colored laser beams that twirled through the club's thick fog. I sensed that each colored ray was an attempt on Steven's part to get my attention. *Meet me backstage*, a blue light said. *I am in need of a wife*, a red light suggested. After the band played their last song, my friend pulled me toward the exit. There was no time to get side-tracked, groupie-style. We had a transaction to make.

I was on a business trip to Boulder, Colorado, delivering these psychedelic mushrooms called *Psilocybe semilanceata*, a.k.a., Liberty Caps. This was a lucrative deal during the fall months, following heavy rains. I lived in Eureka, a small city in the California Redwoods. Every November the city held a mycology festival, and people really got into hunting mushrooms. Since the psychedelic varieties were coveted, a fierce competition arose as soon as the rainy days arrived. The clouds would pile up, the sprinkling would begin, and the first thing I'd do was run to my bedroom to set the alarm clock. If I slept in on hunting day, the patches would be stripped, and my chances for earth-flavored mushroom tea and a few hundred bucks would be as decayed as the fungi's rotting, fleshy caps.

There was this great spot out toward the coast, a clump of shrubs that enshrouded perfectly perky brown shrooms every season, batch after batch— they were so good and fresh, plus the ground my friends and I had to slither across was so dirty in a delicious, pure dirt way. It was the kind of place where we could yank out a carrot and not rinse it off before sticking it in our mouths because the dirt added flavor and minerals.

This special dirt was on private property, so we had to crawl under a wire fence. Everyone would fold up their T-shirts to make a kangaroo-style pouch on their stomach, fill it with mushrooms, then tie it back with twisted T-shirt knots on either side, the kind of knots little girls make when they're imitating Daisy Duke or the Dallas Cowgirls. Since we were belly-bound, we scooched up the pouches like puffy mushroom bras so they wouldn't get crushed. If there were stray mushrooms left on the ground, we filled our hands as we started to crawl away. On the way out, we chucked some leaves over the gap we'd made under the fence, as if we were bunnies sneaking out of a veggie garden. This part was similar to a Peter Rabbit story, but if we'd got caught it would have been more serious, so we didn't fool around.

The limit was three people to a trip, two guys and one girl. I think the guys assumed girls might ruin something. I felt honored when I was along. Gathering shrooms was my favorite thing to do. Plus, on some hunts, I went along with this guy who knew all the species; he'd teach us about Death Caps, the brown ones that looked magic but weren't, the furry, shaggy Ink Caps, and the stunning, red-and-white polka-dotted Fly Agarics (the kind gnomes sit on). I saw caterpillars or titmice hopping around in the branches above our heads, so there was critter magic down there under the tangled twigs. Mushroom world is fairy territory.

Occasionally we drank mushroom tea before we left so we would be more in tune with the shrooms and they could call us to them with their fungus mental telepathy. The guys believed if you drank the tea you could think like a mushroom, which would cause you to gravitate toward the patches. Once I actually thought I had spores so I pictured where I would have dropped mine to reproduce. I imagined what it felt like to live my whole life hidden by leaf debris. The mushroom-thought theory worked so

well that I wondered why anyone would go searching in any other state of mind.

The day after the Flaming Lips show, my friend Jim
and I took a trip to the Denver Natural History
Museum, where we saw Aztec daggers used for cutting out human hearts. One knife had a mushroom-
shaped handle with a little frog crouched on its tip.

"Look at that crazy frog. It's so weird. It's, like,
sitting on a mushroom," I said.

And Jim said, "Cool."

The conversation, which could've been educational
and enlightening, was a dud. I felt like an ignoramus
for not knowing what kind of mushroom the handle
was fashioned after. The Aztecs were expert
botanists; I was sure the mushroom on that ceremo-
nial tool bore great shamanic significance. I was a
poseur, a hippified stoner with a mushroom-amulet
necklace (the swirly colored kind on hemp rope)
who knew nothing about mushrooms except how to
trip out on them. The only minor mushroom knowledge I had, beyond identifying three psychedelic
species in the field, came from Sylvia Plath's poem
"Mushrooms," which has a mysterious, sinister
tone. It's about a mushroom colony breeding
beneath the ground's surface. Plath's mushrooms
grow *Overnight, very / Whitely, discreetly, / Very quietly.* By
the end of the poem, they're powerful, almost evil,
when they tell the reader: *We shall by morning / Inherit
the earth. / Our foot's in the door.*

* * *

On the airplane back to California, I decided if I was going to be into mushrooms, I had to start learning some hard-core scientific information. I purchased David Arora's seminal *All That the Rain Promises and More* . . . a book known by every real mushroom connoisseur. The cover shows a bearded man in a tuxedo holding a cluster of oyster mushrooms and a trombone. Inside there's a picture of a dog whose hair has been dyed with yellow "shroom mush." Right after I got this book, a girlfriend of mine found some Witches' Butter, a rubbery orange fungus that's ruffled like lace and has the chewy texture of seaweed, growing on an oak log. We used the book to identify it. Now we both snap photos of any shelf fungus we locate and mail them to each other for our fungi photo albums.

Thus, my knowledge of the plant kingdom *Thalophyta* can be attributed to that trip to see Aztec daggers. For example, I know that the clumps I used to dig up are known as *thallus*, and the reason the guys told me to pull the mushrooms out by the stems or *stipes* was to preserve the *hyphae* and *mycelium* below, from which new mushrooms can bloom season after season. I also discovered that psychedelic mushrooms are most potent when in a mature stage of fructification and the caps, or *pileus*, are dark-brown and tender.

Clients often ask me what makes mushrooms psychedelic, so I've memorized the molecular structures of psilocybin and psilocin (the chemical that psilocybin breaks down into). Psilocin causes the psychedelic high; scientists think its chemical similarity to serotonin, a natural human neurotransmitter, is what makes psilocin cause hallucinations. Oddly enough, serotonin occurs naturally in the *Panaeolus* genus of mushrooms. Humans share molecules with mushrooms! Perhaps depressed people could eat *Panaeolus* instead of Prozac or Xanax.

Here's a diagrammatic breakdown of the principal active constituents in entheogenic psilocybes. All mushrooms containing these chemicals will produce a blue stain when laid on paper.

Rereading Sylvia Plath's poem now, I feel I should reinterpret her words correctly through a mycological lens. The "toes" and "noses" that "take hold on the loam" are the *carpophores* and *basidiomycetes*, or the fruits and the spores. Her "soft fists" that "insist on heaving the needles" describe gilled fungus in the *button stage* hidden behind their *universal veils*. In a new and exciting way, I love the way Plath's mushrooms *Diet on water, / On crumbs of shadow, / Bland-mannered*, even though that is only a half-truth; *saprophytic* fungi actually require nutrition derived from decaying organic matter, just as the *lignicolous* mushrooms (the kind that live on wood) need that special dirt and log vitamins to thrive and reproduce.

I sometimes wish I could write Plath to explain my discoveries.

One recent Friday night I had some mushroom tea brewed from dried *Psilocybe cubensis* and spent the evening alone.

I can step into a vortex of minutiae. My apartment has teal green walls covered with miniature paintings and small tchotchkes stowed on every shelf. My current favorites are a half-inch-tall ceramic Jawa mounted on a broken cuckoo clock, and a quarter-inch plastic Fly Amanita resting beside a one-inch squirrel holding a mini acorn. One night alone with a mug of mushroom tea can turn this situation into a microcosm of amazement.

After I'd examined the squirrel's hair patterns (the way they swirled in bristly waves over his hindquarters) and its nose, which was smaller than a pinhead yet meticulously tipped in black, Sylvia Plath's book (the one with the mushroom poem in it) started glowing yellow on the bookshelf. It looked as though it were pushing itself off the ledge into my hands. I opened it and proceeded to listen while the poem was read to me in the voice of a woman whom I believed to be Sylvia Plath in the afterlife. Her voice had a low, Lauren Bacall quality. As the poem's lines were recited, I visualized each stanza while making scientifically accurate associations. Each word in the poem—*bedding, hammers, earless, crannies, nudgers*—began to seem like the microscopic reproductive units called *spores*, which are discharged from mushroom gills and dispersed on air currents. The letters that formed the words became akin to mushrooms themselves, which, by the way, are actually the fruits of the fungus—a thing that gives birth to other things.

Life forms such as mushrooms appear immortal because they are basically impossible to eliminate. When you pick a mushroom, the spores that float away will encourage more mushrooms to grow. Dead mushrooms generate life. Look at letters arranged on a page, and they too become a growing puzzle: of words, that is. The more I eat mushrooms, the more I feel related to mushrooms. We both communicate with the dead, in a way.

Sylvia's ghost deduced from my half-formed thoughts that I wished to share my fungi learnings with her. She in turn taught me that words, like mushrooms, are capable of communicating to the living what the dead are trying to say. *Don't write to the dead*, Plath taught me. *We'll come for your thoughts when we want them.* Though I don't sell mushrooms anymore, I do read books written by deceased authors. One can learn a lot from a ghost, and vice versa.

LADY OF THE LAKE

Amy and I pushed our beds together to make an island piled with stiff, green camp blankets and stuffed animals we'd brought from home. We hung by our knees from the headboards and took pictures of each other with monster hair. I looked like the Bride of Frankenstein. She looked hot like a red-faced rock star chugging Gatorade offstage. That's the kind of life I wanted—to be the lady in tight leather pants who wiped her sweat off with a bandana—not the lady cooking chili at our Girl Scout Camp.

We spent Saturday horseback riding, not out on a trail through vines and waterfalls, but in a metal corral. Amy, who was riding behind me, said, "Remember in *Friday the 13th* when the girl gets stabbed in the bathroom?"

We'd been watching horror movies. Amy was a year

older than me, so her mom did the renting. *Friday the 13th, Hellraiser,* and *Repo Man* were the first R-rated movies we saw. We chose them because we liked their boxes. *Repo Man* was boring—something about green glowing stuff and dumb beer guys taking cars away from people for some unknown reason. The others I got into—men gone on killing rampages. I knew a house up the street from mine where the son killed his parents with his dad's shotgun because they wouldn't buy him a Texas Instruments computer.

"Remember that scene when they're playing strip Monopoly and smoking a joint?" I asked, not really knowing what a joint was, much less that strip games were real. I said that extra loud, so the other girls in the corral would hear.

"Last summer I went to a camp that looked just like that one in the movie," Amy said. "The manager had a witch room where he took girls to do spells on and stuff."

I believed her. We'd written several spells ourselves that were effective only when recited while riding our bicycles in circles inside my garage. One went,

Father time,
Father clock,
Make us disappear—
And reappear around the block.

We'd ride our bikes around the block, always winding up in the garage again, then circle the water heater five times while looking down at the ground. The dizziness this induced convinced us that the spell had worked.

"Did he do any spells on you?" I asked, only guessing what kinds of spells a man would employ.

"You wish," she said.

Sunday we swam in the lake. This lifeguard, Rita, caught a rainbow trout. She seemed semi-awesome in her Girl Scout shirt since she'd cut the sleeves off and frayed the edges to look like a metalhead. She removed the hook from its mouth and let us stroke the fish with our index fingers. Feeling the fish made camp less dorky—animals were cool. Raccoons dug through the trash dumpsters, frogs hopped along the creek that ran through commons, and ravens swooped down from the sugar pine trees that circled our cabins. That night we stayed up whispering.

"Did you touch that fish Rita had in her hands?" Amy asked.

"Yeah, it was kind of smelly."

"It reminded me of how tongues are gross."

"I wouldn't know," I said dryly. "You're the tongue master."

"Not even," Amy huffed. She had French-kissed a boy a few months back. "You're the master. You probably practice with your dog."

"I wish," I said. "Dogs are hot."

Amy was quiet. It took her a minute to decide if I was being sarcastic.

Then she turned her flashlight on under her chin. Her face turned red again, only this time it was glowing and eerie, not enviable and sexy.

"Hey," I said. "Remember in *Friday the 13th*, that part at the end where the girl's in the boat after Jason's mom is dead, and Jason comes out of the lake all slimy like he melted in a fire?"

"I do-o-o-o," Amy said, in a not-that-scary ghost voice. "Because that girl in the boat was me-e-e-e."

"I know this sounds stupid, but do you think anyone could live underwater like that? Because when we were swimming today before Rita found the fish, I felt something grab my foot, like a hand." I knew this was hard to believe but it was true.

Amy blinked at me. "It was probably a fish," she said, and switched the flashlight off.

Before school let out for summer, we'd been reading *King Arthur and the Knights of the Round Table.* I liked it because I was sure unicorns would appear in the stories. I figured Guinevere must have had a pet unicorn in the forest somewhere, even if she didn't tell Arthur or Lancelot about it. The Lady of the Lake freaked me out—she came out of the water looking dead but beautiful, holding Excalibur up to Arthur, who was in the boat sailing to Avalon. This woman in a dripping robe convinced me that people could live underwater somehow. I wondered if she'd half-drowned and come back to life, or had gills on her sides that were hidden by her white dress. If that was her in our camp lake, it was okay. Still, I didn't want a lady groping at my ankles while I swam. Also, if that were true, maybe the bottom of the lake was covered with swords poking up. *I'm lucky I didn't get my toes sliced off,* I thought.

It was a three-day-weekend camp. We waited in line for food all Monday morning, then Amy and I headed back to the lake for more fish and swords. She was secretly scared, I could tell. She stayed around the edges, tiptoeing in squishy mud. I was scared too, but I wanted our camp trip to have an R-rating so I'd have stories to tell my friends at school. Watching scary movies made me think my life was dull until something awful happened. Otherwise, I didn't see the point. Otherwise, why would my parents have sent me to this craphole? My need for adventure was half horror movie and half medieval. I wanted to rescue Amy from a mysterious underwater sea hag.

"Come out here," I yelled to the shore.

"No way, it's too cold," she yelled back.

"There's a warm spot," I lied. Then I pictured a shark swimming under me and got a little panicky. "There's a shark out here too," I added.

Amy swam out. I think she took the shark thing as my tease that she was chicken, but I didn't mean that, really.

"This is not a warm spot," she said, paddling her legs furiously to keep her head and neck above water. "I'm swimming over to those plants."

The far side of the lake was thick with lilypads. Dragonflies hovered above them, glittery in the sunlight. No frogs were sitting on the leaves, sadly. Still,

I thought the plants were pretty—they looked like dark, shiny bubbles on the water's surface. I pictured camp counselors canoeing through the lily-pads at night, and I thought how romantic it would be to make out while they shined around the boat.

I followed Amy, staying several feet behind her. The lake was actually quite small, like a large pond. The waves were warm but the deeper parts were cold. I worried there were fish huddling together in the cold parts. I felt them brush against my toes. I pictured the Lady of the Lake—fish skimming over her face, Excalibur glinting in her hand. Just then Amy yelled that she was tangled in the weeds. She splashed around so I knew she wasn't joking.

She was up to her neck in lilypads, and her head looked like some balloon flower. *Pretty flower*, I thought, pushing my way through the watery jungle. I was in a worried daze. When I reached Amy, her legs were so enclosed in vines that I knew I'd have to dive to get her out. She held her breath to stay afloat, puffing out her cheeks, which made her look even more balloon-like.

Once I'd dove down, I knew there was no way to swim back up.

I was too busy struggling to think. But I did see swords surrounding me—which I later realized were only beams of light shining through the lily-pads. Peculiar how swords can be for you or against you—there's no middle ground. Except this time. The swords created an imaginary trap, a cage almost. Then they lit my path upwards. I tried to make myself as tall as possible, then prepared to launch.

Suddenly I was dragged, yanked upwards, and pulled coughing and gagging back to shore. It was the same lifeguard—the semi-awesome one who'd caught the fish.

"Why didn't you two girls call for me earlier?" Rita asked. She wrapped me in a towel and shooed a crowd of girls away.

"I thought I could get her out," I said weakly.

She was buff and blond and sun-tanned and nice, and I was just a little Girl Scout loser. Life had moted me hard. My Lady of the Lake was good not evil, and there was nothing I could do but lie about it.

EXTREME SWEETS

The dog wakes up from a dream at the same time I do. His whimpering wakes me, so I pet his nose to calm him. We were both dreaming about cats. I dreamed that my cat had six kittens, each one a color of the rainbow. The purple one was pastel, the same lavender as the Horse of a Different Color in *The Wizard of Oz* movie. I looked down to see if I was wearing ruby slippers, but I wasn't.

My dog was dreaming of eating cat food. Most of his dreams are about stealing food from other animals. When his paws twitch, that means in his dream he just grabbed some meat and is trying to outrun a pack of vicious, hungry dogs. One time, when he and I were having the same dream, the dogs were faster than him, and I watched them catch up and rip him apart. I woke up crying. I wonder where you go when you die, but mostly I wonder how it affects you when you die in your dreams, night after night. Are you dying a little each time? Your whole life, you're dying, but I try not to think of it that way.

My cousin Laura collects glass animals. She dusts them like forty times per day. When I go over to her house, she constantly glances over to her armoire, making sure her animals are safe.

"What's new?" I ask her.

"Nothing," she says.

"Like a soda?" I ask, tossing her a can.

"Thanks," she says, setting it on the table.

"Want to go to the beach?" I ask.

"Can't," she says. "I'll burn."

"Use sunscreen," I say. "Maybe we'll see dolphins."

She walks over to her shelves and picks up her dolphin. She steams it up with her breath, and polishes it with a diaper cloth.

"Already got one," she says.

"Jesus," I say. "Don't be so melodramatic."

"You're melodramatic, coming over here, all beached up and ready to party."

"What?" I say. "FYI, I'm trying to cheer you up and get you into the sun."

"I get plenty of light," Laura says. "I got these natural lightbulbs on eBay . . ."

"Fuck eBay," I say, then storm out.

I really don't know what's wrong with Laura. She buys and sells animal figurines on eBay so she doesn't have to leave her house. We didn't grow up together.

But she's one of my only relatives. Her mom and my mom are enemies. Laura and I are the same age. She has long brown hair, nice skin and teeth, and she keeps her nails painted. Sometimes when I go over to her house she's in this white gauze gown that looks like it's from Victorian times. I'm sure it's from eBay. I'm grubbier, I shave my head, wear cutoffs, and I keep my nails short so they don't get too much dirt under them. Riding my bike rules my life. I ride my bike around, racing past bums who push shopping carts and ladies who wheel sacks of laundry to the laundromat. Yesterday I saw a lady balancing a box of mangos on her head.

My mom and her sister are enemies because my mom found out that my aunt knew my dad was sick before he died, but she didn't tell anyone. Dad died ten years ago. My mom feels my aunt was partially responsible for my father's death, and my aunt swears that he made her promise not to tell anyone, because he knew he was sick and he would've died anyway. He didn't want everybody worrying about him. But my mom says that doesn't matter, when a man is dying and he doesn't want his wife and kids to know, you tell them anyway. I agree. Not that she killed him, but right after he died I'd lie awake trying to convince myself that my aunt wasn't a murderer. She didn't stab him or shoot him, but she secretly knew he was dying and didn't do a thing to change it. That's pretty close to murder.

* * *

In the middle of the night, my dog and I share candy on the couch. He sits next to me with his paws crossed, staring at my bag of taffy. He's like, *I'll eat it all even if I have to barf it up after.* He's like, *Go For It.* He likes the lime ones; lime is my least favorite. He freaks on sweets. I know it's bad to feed him donuts and Jujubes, but I can't resist. He lives for this. It makes me feel like we're both living our dreams. Sporty, like *Extreme Dreaming!* I imagine myself being interviewed on network television: "I'm just doing the best I can, shedding a little light. Trying to make a difference." Full of slogans, holding my Bit-O-Honey. It's like, you have dreams, night after night, for years on end, they don't make any sense, you wake up, and fuck it—you give your dog a little candy to cheer yourself up. Is that so bad? I mean, is it? I could be thinking of ways to sabotage my will-o'-the-wisp cousin, but no. I just eat candy.

The night after the lavender cat, Laura and I are riding through the sky in a glass elevator, a modern one, not like Willie Wonka's. All four sides of this elevator are made of windows that you can roll down, and the strangers riding with us are hanging out, smoking cigarettes over the edges. I think of what Charlie says in the book—*It's eerie and frightening to be standing on clear glass high up in the sky. It makes you feel that you aren't standing on anything at all.* The sky feels underwater—same blue—and the elevator feels like a glass-bottom boat. It would have been just as surprising to see a hammerhead shark swim past as it is to see this red-tailed hawk flying below the smokers. Things speeding by, like in the tornado before Oz— a cow, a witch on a bike, trees with roots hanging down. Instead though, a hawk and cigarette butts.

Laura shouts, "Come stand on the edge."

"Why don't *you* stand on the edge?"

Laura lights up, and the smoke wafts into my face.

"Blow it out the window," I tell her. As if there aren't windows all around us.

She leans over and whispers, "You know, you could die up here and I wouldn't tell anyone." She gets ready to push me over.

I wake up knowing that if I stayed asleep, I would've died. Basically, I just saved my own life. *Ha!* I think, in the darkness. *You can't kill me!* This applies less to my twisted cousin than it does to the universe. I roll out of bed and into the kitchen, where I pour myself a glass of chocolate milk and drink it in the light of the fridge. It's the ultimate chocolate milk commercial—*Narrowly escaping death, she reaches for the only thing that can satisfy, Milk!*

Next day I go to Disneyland. I feel guilty for leaving the dog home alone all day. "I'll bring you a treat," I tell him, as I pet his head and pull the front door shut.

"He'll be fine," my friend Lois says, putting her sunglasses on. She's an optimist. "Once you ride Space Mountain you'll forget all about him."

"That's true," I say, wondering what Laura's doing. I decided yesterday to stop inviting her out, which also contributes to my guilt. I know from past experience how much it sucks to feel guilty at Disneyland. You're twirling in a teacup at sunset remembering you told your mom you'd cook her birthday dinner; you get off the ride and find a pay phone to call and apologize, but you didn't bring her phone number with you. Harsh.

The Haunted House reminds me of Laura, the painting of the beautiful young girl that morphs into an old hag with snakes in her hair.

"That looks like my cousin," I say to Lois.

"Or you," she jokes.

"Shut up," I say, elbowing her. Still, it's uncanny.

"It's a ride, not a funeral," Lois says.

I remember the glass elevator. "Don't you love Willie Wonka?" I ask Lois.

"We're at Disneyland," Lois says. "Wrong fantasy."

"Let's get candy," I say. When we exit the mansion, we head straight for the stand where I chomp on chocolate turtles and candy canes. I buy Mickey Mouse Pixy Stix for the dog, after I picture his nose dusted with the sugar powder. So cute—canine cocaine. Lois's tongue turns blue as she chews gumdrops. All I can think about is death. Laura, I'm convinced, is trying to kill me with her mind.

"I think my cousin's psychic," I say.

"What?" Lois says.

"Last night, in my dream, Laura was trying to kill me," I explain. "She sits at home all day, tripping out on eBay . . . I feel like right now she's sending me evil vibes."

"No more candy for you," Lois says. "Anyways, you can't die from dreaming about death."

"But she could be willing my demise," I say. "Voodoo."

"Look, Laura might shop too much on eBay, but that doesn't make her a Voodoo priestess," Lois says. "That's, like, from a bad horror movie."

"We'll see," I say. "I better start sleeping with Snickers under my pillow. When I go out, I want to be well stocked."

"There's plenty of candy in heaven," Lois says.

Lois was right: I did eat too much candy at Disneyland. That night my dreams were a mess. I breast-fed a hippo. An albino man with glass teeth stalked me; every time I turned around he was Windexing his grin. My dog spoke backwards, telling me that he needed to be brushed. *Hsurb em,* he said. What's worse, the glass-toothed man finally cornered me at a party, bit my arm with his jagged fangs, and I bled to death while everyone stood around drinking beer.

But Laura wasn't responsible. She had her chance to get in there and damage me, while I was trapped in my sugary nightmares, but instead she stayed up all night haggling, pale-faced in her computer screen's glow.

I get dressed in the morning, grab my favorite thing out of the pantry—King-Sized Reese's—and ride the long orange package over to her on my bike.

"It's 7 a.m.," Laura says as I hug her. "You're sweaty."

"I brought you this," I say, handing her the peanut butter cups.

"Thanks," she says. "Why are you here so early?"

We go inside and she pours me coffee.

"Were you up all night?" I ask. "Doing eBay?"

"Not all night, but for a while. Why?"

"I had a vision of you sitting at your desk, bidding on shit."

"I posted some new animals," she says. "Are you okay?"

"Yeah, yeah. But at Disneyland yesterday, I thought you were trying to kill me," I tell her. "Now I know you're innocent."

"Good," Laura says. "What, are you like taking steroids or something? You're sweating like a horse."

"Fuck it," I tell her. "That's not the point. I realized something. I realized that you may be tweaked, but you're no psychic vampire. I thought about dad. I thought about how your mom kept it secret. It was like she was in the glass elevator. She could see everything going on, she was taking it through the roof, and we just twirled around, like cows in a tornado. Well, that's over. I'm in my own elevator now, and you can't push me out of it!"

"Okay," she says, rubbing her head like she has a headache. She asks, "Were you up all night?"

"No, man, I was dreaming about hippos and glass teeth."

As I hear myself say that, I wonder if I am finally

dead, and if these conversations are the kind dead people have in their dreams. Assuming the dead dream.

A UNICORN-LOVER'S ROAD TRIP

I. Souvenirs

Texas is shaped like a cross. *Love's* gift shops were crosses too, with long, gridlike aisles. Each shop was stationed at a truck stop and had a disco-era, red heart logo. I got lost in *Love's* rows of junk. They were stocked with Lone Star State souvenirs: baseball caps embroidered with farting bulls, leather Texas-shaped key chains, and miniature die-cast metal oil-drilling machinery.

Love's also sold unicorns. They had nonfunctional 3-D sculpted unicorn plates, glass unicorns with gold hooves and horns, and fake jade unicorn carvings imported from China. I guess *Love's* carried these overpriced animals to provide homebound truckers with whimsical trinkets for their wives, girlfriends, and daughters. Their ladies thank, hug, and kiss them, adding the unicorns to their curio shelves. All over Texas, females gaze sentimentally into glass cases crammed with unicorns, reminiscing about the time Dad came home.

Unicorn souvenirs symbolize a man's distance from the women who love him. A unicorn's essential magic is diminished in tacky gift exchanges. My boyfriend Matt gives me unicorns sometimes, but only really nice ones. I can't justify buying pricey souvenirs for myself. Therefore, I only bought unicorn greeting cards. I don't want to become a woman whose house is full of cheap sculpture.

II. Lodging

Matt and I pulled off at a dilapidated roadside motel. Some windows were boarded up, and the walls were stacks of half-painted cinderblocks. But there wasn't another motel for miles. The manager's front porch was a single gas pump. He lived in a gas station. I couldn't imagine his life of constant pumping, dreams and sex interrupted by ringing bells when customers pulled up.

Our room smelled like shit. Old dishtowels were stapled over the windows. A stained mattress hid a powdery pile of cement where construction had halted. A lamp with an insect-hating bulb cast a druggy yellow glow. Porn was the only thing on TV. Our bed was lopsided thanks to squeaky, broken springs.

Lying there, we wondered if our lives were in danger. In the car I'd been horny and now I wasn't. We got dressed, returned the key, and continued driving ganked up on sugary orange-slice candies.

Sixty miles later, we reached a town with a string of motels, and chose one that looked more promising. A patchouli-scented Indian man escorted us to Room 8. Hanging above the bed was a picture of a unicorn and her colt enjoying waterfalls and mist-made rainbows. They stood on an island surrounded by streams and wild ginger plants.

We set down our luggage. My faith in unicorns was renewed. We'd stumbled out of Texas and into paradise. I got horny again thinking of magic horses.

III. The Obsession

I've dreamt of unicorns my whole life. I want one for a pet. Unicorns are real. I see them peering out from behind boulders in the woods. Unicorn-pegasuses fly across full-moonscapes when I stargaze. I count on unicorns appearing when everything goes well. They represent safety and hope.

But I also love raunchy white-trash unicorns. There are lots of them in Texas, mixed among the classic ones. Unicorns reflect the thoughts of people who appreciate them. Fantasy animals manifest human desires.

IV. Gasoline

My main goal on road trips is to avoid running out of gas, so gasoline is always an issue.

When I turned sixteen, I took my first solo road trip to Las Vegas. I ran out of gas and pulled off the highway. A kind man stopped and emptied his red canister into my tank. Another time, I had to drive fifty miles on fumes.

One day in Texas, Matt and I barely made it. We were so relieved to see the giant red heart. When we drove into *Love's*, Matt filled the gas tank and I went inside to pee.

A haggard man eating Flamin' Hot Cheetos leaned against the hot dog display. I remembered a bouffant-sporting poodle lady driving a pink Mary Kay Cadillac back in Dallas. She was eating Cheetos too. Texas seemed junky.

Then a glint of refracted florescent light caught my peripheral vision. A table of tiny crystal unicorns shined and sparkled. They were half-priced from having chipped tails, scratched-up manes, and missing horns.

"You like them unicorns?" the sales lady asked.

"Yeah," I said. "Can I have one for free?"

"Nope," she said.

I wasn't going to pay $6 for a broken unicorn. I went out to the car, got the camera, came back in, and shot some pictures of the unicorn spread. The figurines gave me a reason to be in Texas. Suddenly, I was a unicorn photographer. My truck stop spread could be in a fashion magazine. Unicorns never go out of style. I've got folders full of magazine unicorns. Cameras often capture the magic of mythical creatures. I wanted to document the delicate, rejected horses and give their lives in Texas meaning.

V. Geography

Natural Bridge Caverns' mascot was a slick orange brontosaurus. I expected to see a dinosaur caged in an ornately carved stone pen. Matt and I skipped the Alamo so we could go underground.

Driving to the caves took us through Austrian-style villages landscaped with tulips, windsocks blowing from porches, and cobblestone driveways. Billboards advertised frothy steins of lager. It was a challenge not to pull off the road and get wasted.

At Natural Bridge, opalescent white limestone walls were frosted with thin layers of warm, sulfuric water. Steep, curvy paths lined with colored spotlights gave the caves a kitschy, interplanetary feeling. A "fried egg" stalagmite glowed from red to green when Matt's camera flashed on it. A glossy black heap of bat guano had a brontosaurus shape like one had suffocated underneath it. Silt in the creek beds looked like finely ground white pepper. Blind cave-dwelling shrimp may have been hiding in wet crevices.

As our tour group wound through prehistoric spires and mounds, I noted the majestic names of the formations: *Sherwood Forest*, *Castle of the White Giants*, *King's Throne*. Castle of the White Giants? It was a gigantic room, baroquely decorated with chandeliers, cave bacon, drapery, and other aptly named rocks and mineral deposits. A hump shaped like a harpsichord caught my eye. The 100-foot-high ceiling dwarfed 50-foot stalactites hanging over us. The so-called "white giants" reminded me of unicorn horns.

How many blind shrimp were skewered as those horns emerged during some ancient earthquake?

The ruinous "castle" was a fractured royal home built atop a network of unicorn horns. Tangled, they made a thorny crown on which the palace was balanced. I felt dwarfed imagining skyscraper-sized unicorns living in Earth's mantle. They drilled up to the surface slaying any beast that got in their way. I was scared of unicorns when I had this vertiginous realization of our planet's depths.

VI. Food

Love's sandwiches were disgusting. The turkey was dry and the lettuce was limp. People lined up for food like pigs along a trough.

Fast-food joints lined the highway. Every car was packed with obese people flaunting cigarettes, burgers, and sodas. Dairy Queens in Texas had burgers called "Belt Busters."

Eventually we found a family-owned sandwich shop. The deli workers looked like Def Leppard. It took about twenty minutes to get our lunch, so Matt and I looked at this display case stuffed with hunting knives, switchblades, and handcuffs.

Where there are heavy-metal weapons, there are unicorns. It's a barbarian thing. One dagger had a unicorn head tooled onto its black leather handgrip. The horse looked up at the blade with dedication and reverence. Unicorns elucidate the emotions of weaponry enthusiasts. They can convey macho illusions of grandeur with violent historical periods.

The horn takes on phallic significance. No matter where I am, unicorns clarify the environment. I judge people depending on what kinds of unicorns they have. It might be unfair to remember Texas only by its unicorns, but there were so many—that counts for something.

OCEANIC

At night, paradise is a wilderness. I'm in Maui for a friend's wedding, staying in animal heaven—a hotel where birds, fish, mongoose, snakes, butterflies, lizards, and housecats converge. During the daytime it's sort of like Edward Hicks's friendly painting *Peaceable Kingdom*. At night, turtles skim the sandy ocean bottom for algae and sharks lunge from the water to catch flying fish. I'm lying awake between crisp sheets, paralyzed by underwater fantasies.

All my friends are out skinny-dipping in the surf. I'm starring in *The Shining*. I'm Shelley Duvall, running down the halls trying to escape my psychotic husband. Bloody flash floods and door-choppings are my future.

* * *

When I stay in nice hotels—not the roadside kind—
I get terrified of walking the dark halls alone. Too
many living beings have inhabited them, or have
died in the rooms. For this reason, I have a tendency
to drink too much once I've checked in.

Everyone returns from the starlit swim.

"You should've come," Heidi says. "It was awesome." Of course it was awesome. Everything's awesome because she's about to get married. I sip my
rum and coke.

"I'm not getting in that water at night." I remind
her about the clownfish, puffer fish, brain coral, sea
bass, and purple-spiked sea anemones we saw while
snorkeling yesterday.

"It's the same fish whether you can see them or
not," she says.

Do you ever dream while you're awake? I couldn't
sleep on the red-eye out here, nor last night after six
piña coladas on the beach, following hours of floating through the reef.

The dream: I swim out to meet Heidi, who's treading water under a rocky arch that protrudes from a
deep forest of coral. Crystalline turquoise water carries honeycomb-shaped rods of sunlight hundreds of
feet down. I have my snorkel and mask around my
neck, but I don't want to put them on to see how far
we are from the bottom. It's deep enough for whales
to pass beneath us.

"I'm tired," she says. "I'm swimming back."

As soon as she turns into a speck on the blue horizon, creatures congregate below.

First, the monk seal, whose whiskers tickle my toes as he decides whether I'm something to eat or hump. While he sniffs me, I wonder would it be more foodlike to paddle my legs in a scissoring motion, or coast with no movement as if I were already dead? Next, a school of barracudas arrive to circle under him, their teeth ready to use on his brown leathery flesh. Down below the barracudas appear a pod of gray, rubbery things. And hovering below them, a massive white shadow. There's no way I'll put on my mask. I want to know, but I don't.

The next morning, I put on a sundress and flip-flops, then stop at the café for a muffin and a glass of guava juice—*No rum today*, I think. *Must sleep.* In the chaise lounge area I ask the man sitting next to me what seals eat, and he tells me they eat lots of things.

"They wouldn't eat you, though, unless you were attacking their babies," he says, rubbing coconut oil onto himself.

The bride to be, my best friend, takes the chaise lounge next to mine—I reserved it with my muffin wrapper and sandals—and tells me my feet were twitching while I dozed on the sofa last night.

"A monk seal was about to attack me," I say.

"They don't eat humans," she says, not moving her head from sunbathing position. So the man was right. Heidi knows it all now that she lives on Maui.

"The only predators out there are jellyfish," she says, "and they're clear, so there's nothing you can do."

I hadn't thought of jellyfish.

"I can't sleep," I say. "I keep thinking of that part in *The Shining* where she opens the bathroom window to escape and the snow's blocked her in."

"You're in Hawaii," she says.

When I'm home on the mainland, I go out to the desert sometimes and rent a room by myself. One time I was sitting naked on the bed watching *Three's Company*. It was hardly visible due to bad reception. Green and red lines streaked across Jack and Chrissie's faces. I snacked on some saltines then opened the dresser drawer to check for a Gideon Bible. I read the instruction card for making outside calls, just in case. The air-conditioning froze my stomach when I stood in front of the unit.

I put on my bra, panties, and stockings, to increase my vulnerability. If a pervert were spying on me through my curtains, he would be more likely to strike if he saw me in lacy undergarments, or so movies would have you believe. Naked, I'm pale and blubbery.

When I was in elementary school and first learned about the realities of rape, I remember riding home on the bus from a field trip to Disneyland and wishing I had been dragged into Adventureland, then raped behind Thunder Mountain. Gazing out the window of that reeking, nasty bus, I felt rejected by the imaginary rapist. I wasn't cute or slutty enough. Being slutty was what I aspired to. Bouncing up and down on the black seat helped me imagine being forcibly fornicated by some hairy-chested man. The girl sharing my seat didn't think the rape idea was as sweet as I did; she told me no one ever wants to get raped. I felt stupid for not knowing that. I'd thought it could be fun.

Maybe the monk seal had raped me. He'd sucked on my toes as if they were calamari.

Late in the afternoon, I still haven't fallen asleep. I call my boyfriend back home in California. "Do you ever feel like killing someone?" I ask.

"Of course not," he says. "What are you talking about?"

"I'm so tired I feel like a shark, if that makes any sense. I look around at all these women wearing diamond rings and Gucci sunglasses, and I think they need a little poke. Sharks poke things, right?"

"I guess," he says. "You mean you want to attack them?"

"Yeah, I wish I could shred some people up. But isn't it weird to be scared of attackers when you want to attack?"

"Every man for himself," he says.

I'm assigned bartender duty because at dinner I announced I wasn't going to drink. Why they need a sober drink-mixer is beyond me. I make strawberry daiquiris, papaya margaritas, and mai tais. Another girl pushes maraschino cherries and triangular pineapple slices onto toothpicks. We're in the honeymoon suite, which has a bar built into the mirrored wall. Every time I make a new blender full of fruity stuff, I test it and add more rum. After a while, I have three drinks going on the side at once. I check out my tan in the mirror, thinking, *I like being tan.*

The groom's best man gets out three huge joints. We pretend they're champagne or something and make a toast. The ceremony is tomorrow. *To your life on the island,* we say. *To your life with the monk seal,* I say to myself. There's so much I could learn: is a seal's penis barbed?

I excuse myself and head down to the ocean. I step onto to sand and kick my sandals off into the bushes. The supply rental booth's windows are boarded up but the door is unlocked. I go inside and steal myself a pair of flippers. Flippers will make me more attractive. Maybe seals turn one another on by slapping each other on the ass. Maybe getting slapped feels like a massage. I turn my feet out to the sides to move across the sand without tripping. It's time to swim to my husband.

LOU IN THE MOONLIGHT

I have pleasant dreams in my moon garden. Serenity is key. When I'm sitting on that stone bench beneath the morning glories, nothing stresses me out. My dog's red fur glows like heated copper in the moonlight. He's a buff metalsmith protecting me from worldly harm. He wears a shredded shirt, and beads of sweat dangle off the tips of his red-orange beard as he pounds on his anvil. He has a sword tattooed on his upper arm. He's the perfect bodyguard, the kind of man who will linger in the background and jump out with a machete if anything sketchy happens to me. My dog is the best.

Planting a moon garden isn't difficult. I started when my dog was a puppy and kept me up all night. I needed to occupy myself during the wee hours. Before I got my dog, I didn't sleep well either because in silence my mind takes over. I think too much. Planting datura and nicotiana seemed like the answer. Thus, I dig and weed in my pajamas. When I'm exhausted and dirty from gardening, I can get some rest. Commitment to the plants is the closest I've come to putting down roots. It's like we're married because they depend on me.

"Your garden looks good," my neighbor calls over the fence. I'm gardening and the moon's coming up. *Not just good, lady, magical,* I think. That neighbor bugs me. She's a squat, pudgy troll. She thinks something's wrong because I spend so much time outside at night. My house is tiny. I use the yard as another room. I wear my pajamas because they're comfortable. There's nothing weird about that. I'm nocturnal. This woman looks like an ex-boyfriend I broke up with because he reminded me of Grumpy.

I lie on the stone bench beside my garden like I'm Snow White in a glass coffin. I pretend that dwarves stand around tossing roses at me in mourning. Envisioning myself as Snow White makes me super horny, and lying in my imaginary coffin out in the moon garden is as good or better than having sex. To be quite frank, my moon garden is the horniest place on Earth. I love going there, and so does my dog. If only I had a Prince Charming.

My mom came over for lunch a few weekends ago. She's clueless. She doesn't understand why I like to work at night.

"What's new, dear?" she asked.

"I found this new variety of artemisia," I said.

"Very nice," she said. "Does it smell good?"

"No, it's more for color. It's in the silver section." I pointed out how all the plants surrounding it have silvery leaves.

"Do you want to go shopping?" she asked.

"Is that a hint?" I asked.

"You need some new clothes, you don't have to wear pajamas all the time," she said. "Are you depressed, sweetie?"

"No," I said. "I just like gardening. Does it mean I'm depressed just because I have a beautiful garden?"

"You should date boys," she said. "Instead of working out in the yard all night in an old night-shirt."

She'll never understand. The whole reason I'm designing this yard is to attract the right man.

Lou Reed's *Transformer* plays in the background. *Oh it's such a perfect day / I'm glad I spent it with you.* Cheerfully sad, the way only Lou can do. I lie in my glass coffin waiting for the scents of roses, jasmine, and honeysuckle to permeate that crack where the glass top meets the tomb's marble bottom. My name, *Snow White*, inscribed in cursive upon the marble, is obscured by moss. I've been lying sedately in this greenhouse for a long time. Since I've been unconscious for seasons, I temporarily forget what my name is, then remember it again as I clean the letters. Venus flytraps and other swamp plants grow in here with me, and I'd be eaten alive if it weren't for the most generous sweet peas creeping in. Their curly stems protect me, blooming around my hands folded over my torso. Only once have I felt the flytrap's dewy tendrils snapping closed on a finger. I involuntarily flicked it away.

Besides the plants, there are several flies buzzing around me. They've been trapped in here for ages. They started families in the creases of my dress. Blue velvet serves the maggots well. They build little cocoons; their sticky silk adheres to the dusty fabric. A fairy gave me this dress and I have no intention of letting a few flies ruin it. I've spit bits of that poisonous apple down there to distract them for months at a time. It's funny, I only took one bite but I've spit up perhaps seventy apples worth of fruit. I can't wait until springtime so the glass won't fog up where I breathe.

Even the Prince in *Snow White* doesn't interest me as much as the sparkling gemstones that the dwarves mine. When I do sleep, I dream of rubies, sapphires, and emeralds lining my bedroom walls. That's more comforting to me than having a man in bed beside me. I'm happy to know I can equally love a glamorous cave and a human. Only once did I put the moves on a man in my garden. It was during an intimate dinner party.

I cooked pasta for four friends. Three girlfriends came, and one had a male friend with her who was a motorcycle racer. His name was Pat. He had on a leather jacket. He asked me for a tour of my garden, but I suspected he'd never had respect for plants. He was the kind of guy who would ride his bike through the forest, brutally crushing and killing all the greenery. I found this disturbing but exciting.

The moon was full. We'd just finished another bottle of merlot. Pat didn't seem affected by this but I felt drunk since I hadn't slept well the previous night. I was yawning a lot, and stumbled a couple times.

"This is Angel's Trumpet," I said. "And those are moonflowers."

"Why are you so woozy?" Pat asked.

"I'm just tired," I said. "Let's sit on the bench."

I leaned toward him to see if he smelled good. He smelled delicious in combination with the night-scented flowers that grew on the trellis above us. I invited him to sleep over since he'd been staying at my friend's house for so long. She was getting sick of having a houseguest. They were old friends from back in the day when she used to own a motorcycle herself. One time she'd won him in a race. So it wasn't fishy when he announced as everyone was about to leave that he'd be crashing on the couch at my house. The girls were like, "Good night, Snow White."

The air was crisp and I felt like a moth fluttering around a flower. It was early summer, but I heard the opening sentence of *Snow White* in my head: "It was the middle of winter, and the snowflakes were falling like feathers from the sky." To make myself come, I thought about my bejeweled room. I envisioned lying in a glass coffin. "Satellite of Love's" piano parts played in my head, and Bowie's background vocals transported me to deep space. I looked at my white fingertips coldly burning from gripping my stone bench so hard. I thought of Snow White, icily dormant, cursed with the Sleeping Death. I pretended I had chipmunk friends to sing to. I saw white stripes lining their backs, fuzzy little landing strips. I saw baby chipmunks running in and out of their hole, each one pausing to rub noses with the next one as in some cozy mountain love film. Bluebirds whistled to me and I whistled back. When I opened my eyes all the flowers seemed pointed right at us; there were bright blooms everywhere. The garden looked incandescent glowing with moonlight. Everything went white as I came, as if the moon suddenly got brighter.

Pat slept on the couch. I woke him up and gave him coffee. I thought a lot about hearts. I wondered why they're associated with love, and wondered why mine didn't seem either elated or broken. I cooked bacon for breakfast, started thinking about eating pigs, and realized the link between pigs and hearts: the evil queen. "It was salted and cooked," *Snow White* goes, "and the wicked woman ate it up, thinking that there was an end of Snow White." What would possess somebody to eat a heart? If I hated someone I still wouldn't eat their heart. It's bad enough to eat a pig's hind legs. My mom used to feed chicken hearts to our dogs. The heart symbolizes the place love comes from, but biologically it functions as a pump for blood. When I consider blood and love commingling, I think of an aroused man. The plants' stems get hard as I water them. Watering plants is a feminine thing to do. Consuming another person's organ is a female idea. I got horny as I ate the bacon.

My mother works full-time as an accountant, and sometimes I wonder if she's jealous of the satisfaction I get from gardening in my PJs. Everything she says to me sounds like criticism. *You're too old to be lounging around all day*, she tells me. *Dress up*, she says. *Get out there and earn some money. Stop looking like a peasant so you can meet a man. It's unhealthy to socialize with plants*, she says. She's required to wear suits and nylons to work, and she never leaves the house without first applying lipstick. Since she's single, pretty, and in her fifties, lots of older men ask her out. She goes to see movies with them but rarely finds them interesting enough to continue dating. That's where we see eye to eye.

"How was your evening with Lee?" I ask her on the phone.

"He took me out for Italian," she says. "He ordered one big plate of spaghetti and wanted us to share it. So corny. Did you do anything fun this week?"

"I mulched," I tell her. "That guy Pat called, but I didn't call him back."

"I don't want you going out with men who ride motorcycles," she says. "They're too dangerous."

"I don't want you dating men who make you share spaghetti," I say.

It's unclear to me what benefits come from working all the time in a lousy office and dating nerdy bachelors. I'd rather be broke and stay home with the plants. During the daytime, I occasionally write articles for gardening magazines; I slide by on that meager income. One time I was hired as a hostess at a restaurant, but when the manager asked me to put on makeup and a shorter skirt for my next shift, I quit. Plants don't care what I wear. I aim to sleep all day and wake up around sunset.

My dog and I will wait for Lou. I'll invite him over on a full-moon night. Lou will pet the dog when he walks out to my backyard. As I hand him a glass of wine, he'll notice my gown, feeling the soft yellow ribbon tied around my waist. All the white flowers will open up and face us. A bunny will jump into Lou's lap as he sits down on the bench with me. A doe will trot up and lick my hair smooth again after Lou puts his hands all through it. We'll tie the knot, then Lou will take me to the castle he bought thirty years ago after he had a drug-induced vision of Snow White loving him.